VICTORIAN
MANSION
FLOWER SHOP™
MYSTERIES™

Suspicious Plots

Jolyn Sharp

Annie's®

AnniesFiction.com

Books in the Victorian Mansion Flower Shop Mysteries series

Suspicious Plots
Copyright © 2018, 2021 Annie's.

Library of Congress-in-Publication Data
Suspicious Plots / by Jolyn Sharp
p. cm.
I. Title
                    2018909350

AnniesFiction.com
(800) 282-6643
Victorian Mansion Flower Shop Mysteries™
Series Creators: Shari Lohner, Janice Tate
Editor: Elizabeth Morrissey
Cover Illustrator: Bob Kayganich

10 11 12 13 14 | Printed in China | 9 8 7 6 5 4 3

1

The delicate scent of lavender wafted through the air, and Kaylee Bleu inhaled appreciatively. Summer had certainly arrived in Washington's San Juan Islands, and the herb's purple blooms extended in a vibrant panorama in the field behind Kaylee's home, Wildflower Cottage. As she exhaled, she turned her attention back to the discussion heating up among her friends.

"So you're saying these books are like *The Lord of the Rings*?" Kaylee asked, arching a skeptical eyebrow at DeeDee Wilcox. "I have to confess that I'm not big into dragons and fairies."

"Everybody said they weren't into adolescent wizards before Harry Potter," DeeDee replied with a shrug. "And look how that turned out."

Jessica Roberts raised her glass of iced tea. "Hear, hear."

"I can't keep the Books of the Night series in stock." DeeDee owned Between the Lines, a mystery bookstore in their beloved hometown, Turtle Cove, on beautiful Orcas Island. "They're like J. R. R. Tolkien meets Agatha Christie."

"Just imagine how popular they'll be once the television series comes out," Jessica added. "I hear there's one in the works."

"You've read these too, Jess?" Kaylee asked.

Jessica nodded. "And I enthusiastically second DeeDee's recommendation."

Mary Bishop chimed in. "I read an article saying that these books are all the rage on college campuses these days."

"Well then," Kaylee said with a smile, "if they're what all the cool kids are reading, how can I refuse?"

"Admit it, Kaylee—resistance is futile." DeeDee pulled a

somewhat battered hardcover book out of her tote bag and handed it to Kaylee. "You've got to at least try the first book in the series."

"If this is the first one, why is it called *The Night of the Third*?" Kaylee asked.

"You'll find out," DeeDee replied with a smile.

Kaylee flipped the book over and gazed at the photograph of the impossibly young author on the back. "So this Griffin Graves is coming to Turtle Cove?" she asked. "And teaching a workshop? That sounds like quite a commitment."

DeeDee's beaming smile proclaimed her pride in securing this coup for her bookstore. "He lives on the mainland, but he's staying on the island for the week. Few can resist Moira's place." DeeDee's friend Moira Harper owned a gorgeous second home in one of the most spectacular spots on Orcas Island, but the travel photographer was rarely there. When DeeDee needed an incentive to tempt the occasional famous author to the island, Moira often happily donated it as a guesthouse, a lure that frequently helped seal the deal.

"I'd stay there for free while I spend a week being fawned over by my biggest fans," Jessica said. "Not exactly a hard sell."

DeeDee chuckled in agreement. "The workshop filled up in record time. And I think some of the students are so eager that they're already in town. I arranged a special rate for them at the Tall Pines B&B."

"That's a good choice," Mary said. "Conrad is an excellent chef."

"Speaking of which . . ." Jessica leaned over to peer around Mary. "How are those hamburgers coming, gentlemen?"

On the other side of the deck, four men were clustered around a grill. Mary's husband, Herb, wore a striped chef's apron, but it was DeeDee's husband, Andy, who wielded the spatula. Andy managed a natural-foods store, and he and DeeDee had brought over grass-fed ground beef, fresh corn on the cob, and locally made ice cream. They'd also brought their school-age daughters, Zoe and Polly, who were in the yard tossing a tennis ball for Kaylee's dachshund, Bear.

"Yeah, Dad," Zoe, the older of the girls, said. "We're starving. And so's Bear. Right, buddy?" When Bear gave a yip, Polly threw the ball again, and he dashed after it as fast as his little legs could carry him.

"They're coming along," Luke, Jessica's husband, called out, then turned back to the conversation he was having with local handyman and handsome bachelor Reese Holt.

Jessica chuckled as she picked up the sweating iced tea pitcher and refilled everyone's glasses. "That's Luke code for 'it will be a while,'" she said authoritatively.

"I'm in no hurry," Kaylee said, leaning back in her chair with a sigh. "I'm beat. The twelve-hour days are beginning to wear on my old bones."

"Careful." Mary wagged a finger at Kaylee, but there was a twinkle in her eye. "We're all your age or older." As Kaylee's part-time help at her florist shop, The Flower Patch, Mary had been working those long hours right alongside her, courtesy of tourist season on the island.

"Whatever age my bones are, they're aching too," Jessica agreed. She owned Death by Chocolate, the bakery next door to The Flower Patch, and her business was benefiting from the recent influx of tourists and summer residents as well. "Not that I'm complaining. We're on track for a record summer, and it's barely begun."

"Same here, fingers crossed," Kaylee said. "I hope the Fourth of July Festival planning committee likes the red, white, and blue window boxes we did."

"How could they not?" Mary asked. "They're spectacular, if I do say so myself."

"Have you had much luck with your new idea of renting out big potted plants?" DeeDee asked Kaylee. "The ones you brought over to the bookstore are just the thing I needed to create a private area for the workshop."

"It was hardly my idea," Kaylee said modestly. "You're the one who asked me for help creating a partition, and Mary was the one who suggested plants."

"Whoever's idea it was, they're perfect." DeeDee took a sip of iced tea. "What are they called again? Monster trees?"

"*Monstera deliciosa*," Kaylee corrected with a chuckle. "I chose them both for the name and for the fact that the broad leaves will offer plenty of privacy for your budding authors."

"Clive Randall sure seemed impressed when he saw you arranging them," DeeDee said.

"So impressed that he asked Kaylee to come to his gallery Monday for a consultation," Mary added.

"Really?" Jessica's warm brown eyes lit up. "Half the artwork in his gallery costs more than my car. He's definitely someone whose good side you want to be on."

"He wants some tall plants to add atmosphere during an upcoming event," Kaylee said. "It's a retrospective of paintings by Shirley Lucas, that regional artist who passed away recently."

"The burgers and corn will be ready in ten minutes, ladies," Reese called from the grill.

"I guess it's time we start doing our part," Kaylee said as she scooted her chair back. "I'll grab the condiments."

"I'll come with you," Mary volunteered as she got up. "My salad is in the fridge."

"I'll do drinks," Jessica offered.

"My helpers and I will set the table," DeeDee announced, then said to her daughters, "Girls, let's go wash hands."

A short while later, the group of ten—plus Bear, who sprawled at Kaylee's feet with his head on her foot and hope in his big brown eyes—had gathered around the large patio table. As Kaylee took a bite of her hamburger, she marveled at how life's journey had brought her to this moment, sharing a Saturday evening cookout with close friends she hadn't even known just a couple of years before.

Formerly a professor of plant taxonomy at the University of Washington and occasional forensic botanist with the Seattle police, Kaylee had been laid off in a department reshuffle. With her professional life turned upside down, she moved from Seattle to Turtle Cove to take over The Flower Patch from her grandmother, Bea Lyons, who had retired and moved to Arizona. She had also taken Bea's place in the Petal Pushers garden club, where she'd become close with fellow members Mary, DeeDee, and Jessica.

Mary's kind voice broke into Kaylee's thoughts. "I love what you girls did with the table lighting," she was telling Polly and Zoe. "I'd have never thought to put citronella candles into jelly jars."

Jessica nodded in agreement. "I love how the candlelight glows through the textured glass. It's absolutely magical."

"It reminds me of the dragon lights of Ellaryn in *The Night of the Third*." Zoe was clearly quite proud that she'd recently read her first "grown-up" book. The preteen glanced around the table and asked in a mature voice, "What are you all reading this summer?"

"Funny you should ask," Herb said, a twinkle in his eye. "I'm in the middle of a book about the development of the American power grid. I bet it's right up your alley, Zoe."

Zoe made a face that suggested it wasn't and turned to Luke. "Are you reading anything right now?"

Luke scratched his chin. "Let's see, I just finished Ty Cobb's memoir, and now I'm reading a book about Jackie Robinson." At Zoe's blank expression, Luke explained, "They're great baseball players."

Zoe just nodded and moved on to the next adult. Aside from Kaylee, who was well into a mystery set in the Roaring Twenties, and Polly, who had just begun the fourth Harry Potter book, everyone else seemed to be starting, finishing, or in the middle of a Griffin Graves book. DeeDee said she was rereading the series ahead of her workshop, and Andy admitted that she'd gotten him hooked as well. Jessica, too, had been reading the Books of the Night, which she claimed her twentysomething daughter, Mila, had first brought to her attention.

Kaylee wasn't surprised by the others, but when Reese said that he was just starting the second book in the series, she shot him an incredulous look. "Really? You too?"

He threw up his hands and laughed. "What can I say? Even the island handyman likes a well-written adventure. You've got to give them a chance, Kaylee."

"But there are dragons," she protested.

"Dragons and much more." Reese paused. "But I don't want to give you any spoilers."

Kaylee sighed. "And you promise there's a mystery buried in the fantasy?"

"The mystery generates the momentum of the plot, and there's a huge emphasis on plant life, though it's largely fictional," Jessica said. "You'll love it. Trust us."

"I suppose I could crack into it tomorrow after church." Considering how busy they'd been at the flower shop, Kaylee had intentionally left her Sunday open so she could relax a bit before returning to the shop's hectic seasonal pace on Monday.

"Attagirl." DeeDee beamed at her. "If you don't like the one I gave you, we'll stop harassing you. But I'm betting you'll be banging down my door for the next one as soon as you hit the last page."

Jessica and Mary raised their iced tea glasses to that, and the group fell into quiet contemplation. In the silence, the tree frogs started their rhythmic calling. Kaylee peeked under the table and saw that the evening's sounds had lulled Bear to sleep.

After a delicious dessert of brownies from Jessica's bakery topped with scoops of the ice cream the Wilcoxes had brought, the party broke up.

"We'd better get these two girls home to bed," DeeDee said, standing. Zoe joined her, and Andy gently lifted a sleepy Polly in his arms. "This was lovely. Let's do it again—maybe at the end of the season, when we all come up for air again."

"Thank you all for coming," Kaylee said as she rose to bid her guests farewell. "It really was a perfect evening."

"I'll see you next Saturday to fix that sticky door at the shop," Reese said.

"You're on," Kaylee replied.

Mary hugged Kaylee. "And I'll see you Monday morning, bright and early."

One by one, the guests said good night, until it was just Kaylee and Bear left on the deck. When it was silent once more, the tree frogs resumed their singing.

2

The sun had barely peeked over the horizon when Kaylee and Bear entered The Flower Patch Monday morning, and Mary arrived right behind them. While Bear, who sported a jaunty red bow tie with blue anchors on it that morning, curled up with a chew toy on his dog bed, Kaylee and Mary worked together on a few special orders as well as some patriotic bouquets for the sales floor.

They made half a dozen of the arrangements, which featured creamy white and red roses interspersed with blue *Centaurea cyanus*—known commonly as cornflowers or bachelor buttons—but once Kaylee had flipped the door sign to *Open*, the beautiful bouquets were sold out within the hour. By lunchtime, Kaylee had a list of five more customers who wanted similar arrangements, and she'd promised them they'd be done the next day. *I sure hope my next wholesale shipment is on time this afternoon,* Kaylee thought.

Checking the time after her last customer, Kaylee saw that she had only a few minutes to clean herself up before her appointment with Clive Randall. After washing her hands and checking to make sure that her straight, dark hair was behaving, she left the shop in Mary's hands and headed down to the Randall Gallery, which was located at the end of the Turtle Cove business district. The building that housed the gallery sported a corner entrance, surrounded by large windows that caught the diffused light coming off the water, and the interior's white walls offered an airy and open space to hang and view art. A narrow alley ran along the side of the building, leading to a rear parking lot.

Clive Randall was standing next to a ladder, directing an assistant in hanging a rather large painting, when Kaylee opened the door and set off a subtle chime. A small man dressed somewhat formally for Turtle Cove in summer-weight wool slacks, an Oxford shirt open at the collar, and a vest, he had sandy hair flecked with gray and cut in a youthful style. He turned and greeted her warmly when she stepped in.

"Miss Bleu, I am so honored that you have given us your time today," he said, reaching out to shake her hand.

"Kaylee, please."

"Only if you'll call me Clive. Let me give you a tour."

"I'd love one," Kaylee said.

"Hannah, I'll return shortly," Clive told his assistant, then gestured for Kaylee to follow him from the large front room down a hallway. "This building used to be a five-and-dime store, if you can believe it."

"It's certainly much different now," Kaylee said, noting the gallery's modern, minimalist style.

"There's an office and a framing workroom off this hallway, plus our rear exit, and then we have another gallery at the back." Clive pointed toward a darkened doorway at the end of the hall.

As they passed the workroom, Kaylee caught sight of large, stretched canvases draped with cloth. She assumed these were paintings awaiting their frames. When they entered the rear gallery, Kaylee squinted in the darkness at a series of portraits. When Clive flicked the lights on, however, Kaylee saw not people but plants. Peering more closely, she realized that each painting's subject was presented in a manner that recalled traditional portrait poses.

"Shirley Lucas called this her Still Life series, but" —Clive swept his arm around in a circle—"there is so much energy in these paintings. I'd hardly call them still. You can almost feel them breathe."

"They're beautiful, and yet they sort of make me want to laugh." Kaylee felt a little embarrassed at not being appropriately reverent in a room filled with art.

"I think that was the artist's intent. Shirley Lucas infused her world with whimsy." He stepped toward a painting and waved for Kaylee to come closer. "Look at the detail she gave to the leaves, the pots. She studied everything, and yet in capturing a true likeness of such familiar subjects, she managed to make them . . . strange."

"And breathtaking. That's a *Dracaena marginata*, a dragon tree. It's a common plant for an office, but here it has so much personality. It's almost winking at me."

Clive laughed. "Actually, that leads me to what I was hoping to consult with you about." They moved to the next painting. "From what I can gather from interviews and the few scholarly articles about Shirley's work, this series features common houseplants. Most of the paintings in the other room are from another phase, in which the artist was capturing plants that grow wild in the Pacific Northwest region."

As Clive spoke, Kaylee made her way around the room, examining each painting and gauging the expressions of the plants depicted. By the time she came full circle, she was utterly charmed by the series.

"What I'd like," Clive said when she rejoined him, "is to place some live plants about the gallery that would complement these painted ones."

Kaylee nodded thoughtfully and bent over to read a price tag. When she saw the figure, her eyes widened and she stood up again. "Do all of her paintings cost around that much?"

"Some more, some less." Clive shrugged. "It's been a slow process, but at last her popularity is growing. Not everything displayed here is for sale. I've managed to convince a few of my clients who own her works to let me display them for the show. They agreed because a retrospective will raise her profile, and thus the value of her work." Clive sighed. "It's such a pity she was all but unknown while she was alive. I should know. I represented her from the beginning, as she started painting rather late in life."

"What about her family? Do any of these pieces belong to them?"

Clive gazed at the paintings on the wall. "Sadly, no. They've lost almost all control of her work by now. Although her grand-children came to me recently for help reclaiming a few pieces, if possible."

"Is that difficult?"

"It can be. Come this way. I want you to see some other pieces," he said, waving Kaylee out of the back gallery.

She followed Clive down the hall to the front gallery, where she realized that the room was only partially ready for the event. Here, the paintings were even larger, and the plants depicted were shown in their natural landscape. As Kaylee examined the artworks more closely, however, her sense of unfamiliarity increased. They were all still familiar plants—albeit with a higher concentration of more exotic varieties—but the artist had succeeded in making the familiar feel strange, just as Clive had said. In the way that the other paintings imbued the plants with human characteristics, in these examples they appeared almost animal-like. She glanced at Clive, who seemed to anticipate her question.

"From what I understand, it may be hard to find suitable companion plants for this series," he said. "But I'd be very interested to see what you come up with."

Plants and paintings in dialogue. What a lovely idea. Kaylee smiled. "I would love to help. Do you mind if I take some quick photos to help me remember what's here?" She pulled out her phone.

Clive hesitated. "They must be strictly for your personal use," he said. "I don't have the rights to reproduce these works, and photographs would be a form of reproduction."

"Of course," Kaylee agreed. She quickly took photos of the paintings in both galleries, then returned to her client. "And now, let's talk about what else you might like for the gallery."

"I'm all ears," Clive said.

She gestured toward the front door. "*Howea forsteriana* are elegant door framers, and they can mark a transition from the world outside to the world that Shirley Lucas created with her art. And then perhaps a *Dracaena marginata* about four feet high to draw attention to the hall. That might help unify the two series."

"Lovely. What's a—what did you call it?"

"Oh, the *forsteriana*? Those are the Kentia palms. I have two right now that are just over five feet tall. I can have them ready for delivery by tomorrow morning." She outlined some additional options, and Clive seemed pleased with her proposal.

"Perfect," he said when they'd covered the entire gallery. "It's all coming together so nicely. Promise me that you'll come to the opening reception. You can meet the artist's grandchildren."

"I'd love to. Thank you for the invitation."

Clive beamed at her. "It's really going to be special."

Kaylee returned his smile as she said goodbye, but in her mind she was running the numbers. *How much extra business would I have to do to buy one of Shirley Lucas's paintings?*

That afternoon, after Kaylee had sent Mary home to relax, Bert Greenleaf dropped by The Flower Patch with his Jack Russell terrier, Rocky. Bert owned A New Leaf, an interior design shop in Turtle Cove that he ran with his wife, Ingrid.

"Judy Pratt showed my wife the bouquet she bought this

morning, and Ingrid sent me over here right away to order three of them for the shop," he told Kaylee. "I know you're busy, and I wouldn't bother you if she didn't have her heart set on them."

"No bother at all. It's always a pleasure to see you, Bert," Kaylee replied.

"A glassblower on the mainland has created blue-and-white starburst vases exclusively for us to sell. Those arrangements will be just the thing to show them off. Rocky, no!" He interrupted himself to chastise his energetic dog, who'd gotten a hold of one of Kaylee's foam cylinders and was running around the shop followed by Bear.

Kaylee managed to entice the two playful dogs to the sitting room with Bear's squeaky rabbit toy, then shut the door on them. Bert and his wife were regular customers, and Rocky was one of Bear's best friends. The dogs would be fine in there together.

Kaylee returned to the front counter, where Bert was waiting. "We'll have your arrangements ready for pickup tomorrow morning, if that works for you." Kaylee rubbed her temples. "I just need to find a moment to make them."

"We've been slammed over at the shop too. A nonstop flow of foot traffic. Including . . ." Bert paused, checked to make sure no one else was listening, then leaned toward Kaylee. "We had a notorious character drop in, and I suspect he's making the rounds. Again."

"Who? What happened?"

"A wheeler-dealer by the name of Baron. Have you encountered him?"

Kaylee shook her head, intrigued.

Bert pursed his lips, and Kaylee suddenly had a very good idea of exactly how he felt about the man. "Emmet Baron. He's one of those guys that always has some scheme going. I mean, he seems to have a legitimate business as a publisher.

That's over on the mainland, and I guess he's done a lot of regional-interest books. I don't know much about that." He glanced about again. "He has a house here on the island, up on Mount Constitution. But any time I've seen him in Turtle Cove, it seems he's peddling another scheme."

Kaylee furrowed her brow. "You mean things that are illegal?"

Bert hesitated. "No, I wouldn't say that. There just always seems to be something off about them—and him. The last time he came to my shop, he had this set of plastic toy monsters that he claimed were collectible. He said I should sell them for fifty bucks each. They were obviously junk, and I'm not sure why he even brought them to me. I don't deal in that sort of thing. It still took me two hours to get rid of him, and he had the nerve to get a little nasty with me at the end. I was worried I'd have to call the police."

"He sounds more than just persistent," Kaylee said.

"I'll say. There's something about him that just makes your skin crawl." Bert's voice had risen in his indignation, but he lowered it once again. "And I'm not saying I know anything for certain, but he has a reputation for reneging on commitments and not paying his bills. Granted, I've only heard those things through the grapevine. Wouldn't surprise me, though."

"Goodness," Kaylee said, not sure how to respond to Bert's speculation about a man she didn't know.

"To tell you the truth, after the last time, I was surprised he had the nerve to even come to my shop, not that it seemed to bother him any. He breezed right on in as if nothing had happened. But I hadn't forgotten. I ran him out as soon as he opened his briefcase."

Kaylee had always found Bert very friendly, so she was startled by the satisfaction in his voice. "You mean he's back with something new?"

Bert shrugged dismissively. "Note cards, apparently. He's always got something on offer, but it always comes with a price." He straightened. "Anyway, I just wanted to give you a heads-up. The man's a pest. Give us a call if he comes at you and won't take no for an answer."

"Thanks," Kaylee said, appreciating the support within the small-business community in Turtle Cove. Suddenly, Kaylee felt that the shop was a little too quiet. "What do you think those dogs are up to?"

With Bert close behind, Kaylee went to the sitting room and opened the door to let them out. They found Bear and Rocky playing tug-of-war with one of the couch pillows. Thankfully, it appeared the only damage done was a little slobber on the fabric.

"Rocky!" Bert snapped his fingers. "Come!" The little Jack Russell immediately released the pillow and followed his master out the front door.

Kaylee glanced down at Bear. "Well I hope you had fun."

In response, Bear trotted to his bed behind the counter, where he flopped down for a nap in spite of the bustle around him.

During a brief lull in the late afternoon, Kaylee thought she'd have a chance to sit down in the kitchen for a snack. But she'd no sooner peeled the lid off a plastic container of blueberry yogurt than she heard the door chime, followed by shoes scraping against the shop's wooden floor. Bear was first to dash out and greet the customer, but the short, square-faced man didn't seem to notice the little brown dachshund at his feet as he marched straight to the counter and rapped his knuckles on it.

Concerned that he could be a disgruntled customer, perhaps a father of a bride who wasn't happy with the cost or quality of the wedding arrangements, Kaylee hurried over.

The man's posture softened when she approached. "Kaylee Bleu, I presume? Just the woman I wanted to see."

"How can I help you?" Kaylee asked, trying to hide her relief that he wasn't an irate client.

"The name's Emmet Baron," he said, now smiling broadly. "And have I got something to show you."

3

The man standing before Kaylee was short and stocky, and his bushy eyebrows nearly met below his receding hairline. When he smiled, his eyes narrowed and creased at the outside. It was a charming feature, and Kaylee wished Bert Greenleaf had let her form her own conclusions about this man's character.

"Yes?" she prompted.

With a wink, he held up his index finger. As he did so, his sleeve slipped down to reveal an expensive gold watch. Kaylee took note of his casual but expensive-looking attire, from his sweater vest to his tassel shoes. He had the appearance of a professor, albeit a wealthy one.

Emmet pulled out a large, waxed-paper envelope from his briefcase and extracted three note cards. He fanned them out on the counter.

Kaylee immediately recognized the work of the artist being celebrated at Clive's gallery, Shirley Lucas. She gave Emmet a quizzical gaze.

He cleared his throat. "Now I don't know if you're an art lover, though I have to think that a dealer in floral beauty surely must be." He paused, but Kaylee didn't respond. Undeterred, Baron nodded and continued. "I thought so. And you may know that this artist is a hot ticket right now." He tapped the cards with a finger.

"Shirley Lucas, you mean?"

"That's her name. Well, was, I should say. Sadly, she's deceased, but she spent her life in the region. She's a local artist, and she often visited Orcas Island, I'm told. She was Native

American too—an enrolled member of the Makah Tribe." His voice took on a confidential air as he said, "And that is money in the bank."

He paused again for effect, but Kaylee, who herself had some Native American ancestry by way of her father, declined to agree with him. Instead, she asked, "What is it I can do for you, Mr. Baron?"

He assumed a more conversational tone. "You know the Randall Gallery here in town, I imagine?"

"I do."

"Well, I've been working with them on a major exhibit of Lucas's paintings. I own a number of her works, you see, and I'm making it my mission to get the word out about her."

To increase the value of your own investment, Kaylee thought to herself, recalling the prices she had seen on the works in Clive's gallery. She was beginning to think Bert had been right about this man.

While Emmet had been talking, a young couple had wandered in and begun browsing very casually—a sign that they probably wanted to consult about custom arrangements. She craned her neck to try to see her customers, but Emmet ignored her body language and upped the volume of his voice.

"My day job is book publisher," he continued. "Puget Press, over on the mainland. I also have a house here on the island. So you see, I'm a local too, and I do what I can to support the local artistic community."

The name Puget Press rang a bell, but he kept talking before Kaylee could place it.

"As I said, I've got this exhibit going. The opening is tomorrow night, by the way." He gave her an inquiring gaze, and Kaylee nodded to indicate that she was aware of the event. "I'm also putting together a book, a major retrospective of Shirley's work.

And I've had these special note cards done up in a very limited run. I'm only giving the finest businesses in the area a chance to carry them."

At last, he paused long enough for Kaylee to examine the cards. They appeared to be more of the plant portraits she'd seen at Clive's gallery, though something about them nagged at the back of her mind. The printing was adequate and the card stock likewise, but it wasn't the mediocre quality of the product that was bothering her. She tried to recall whether she had seen these particular images at the gallery, and then with a start, it hit her. *I can't name these plants.*

Given her years of training, it was second nature to Kaylee to identify and categorize any flora that she came across. Even with the stranger of the two series at the gallery, she had still recognized the plants. But with these, it seemed that the more she looked at them, the more elusive the identifications became. The moment her unconscious sorting mechanism was about to slot one of the plants into its proper Linnaean category, it would snag on some uncharacteristic feature that would negate the classification. Her eyes roved restlessly over the cards, desperately seeking some purchase of certain identification. Lucas's paintings offered sufficient detail, even in these reproductions, and Kaylee's inability to put their names to these plants gave her an unsettled sensation she found quite unpleasant.

It was only the ring of the bell as the young couple departed that broke the spell and allowed Kaylee to take a mental step back, abandoning her effort to identify the plants.

Baron apparently read her absorption as commercial interest. "As you can see, there are three designs, and each box has four each for a total of twelve cards. I'll sell them to you for half the set list price. I'd be happy to discuss an appropriate volume discount." He gave a satisfied smile. "What do you think?"

Still feeling slightly off-balance, and annoyed that she'd been unable to help the couple that had left, Kaylee asked, "Are these paintings part of the gallery exhibit?" She couldn't remember seeing them, but she wanted to be sure.

"No," Baron said quickly. "These are some from my personal collection that I have no intention of selling." His next words sounded almost sly. "They're special to me."

Kaylee thought of Clive's comment when she had asked to take pictures at the gallery. In turn, that made her recall a dinner party that she'd attended years before, back when she was still teaching at the university. There had been a number of young faculty members there from a variety of departments. One of the guests had been a particularly interesting young woman from Art and Design who had described at some length the complicated rights questions involved in the sale and reproduction of paintings by contemporary artists. Kaylee quite clearly remembered the woman's assertion that mere ownership of a painting did not necessarily give someone the right to commercialize the image—for instance, by printing up cards or T-shirts and selling them.

"So these are from your personal collection," she said slowly.

"That's right."

"And you also control the reproduction rights then?"

Baron's smile wavered for just a fraction of a second. "Of course, of course. As I say, they're my paintings."

Kaylee's gaze drifted back down to the note cards, but Baron suddenly seemed eager to wrap up.

"I'll tell you what, you think it over, okay?" He hurriedly scooped the cards off the counter, then stuffed them back into his briefcase and closed it up. He was already heading toward the door when he said, "I'll be in touch. Have a good day."

And he sailed out of the shop.

The next day, Kaylee was still haunted by the plants depicted on the note cards—and by her inability to identify them. The evening before, she had spent some time with her reference books, looking up the plants they most closely resembled. Maybe the images depicted some unusual variant she just happened not to know. But if that was the case, then they were variants also unknown to the experts who compiled her references.

She had also gone online and done a search for Shirley Lucas. She had found images for only a few of her paintings, most of which she recalled seeing at Clive's, but she didn't find any of the images on the note cards. She began to wish that she had asked Emmet Baron for a sample set so that she could study them more closely, even though it would have been a request made under false pretenses. She strongly suspected that Emmet did not have the right to produce and sell those cards, and if that was the case, she certainly was not going to carry them in her shop.

But she had learned a fair amount about Shirley Lucas, who appeared to have been a strongly self-directed and rather whimsical individual, both as a person and an artist. Even before her death the previous year, Lucas's reputation had been on the rise, and now it seemed to be skyrocketing. Kaylee thought sadly of the family Shirley had left behind—an ex-husband and some grandchildren—and how her posthumous popularity must be quite bittersweet.

The images on the note cards continued to pop unexpectedly into Kaylee's head all morning as she finished the bouquets for Bert and Ingrid, then gathered up the plants for the event at the Randall Gallery. She got them delivered and set up by late morning, and then returned to assist Mary with filling orders and helping customers.

Wanting a distraction during an afternoon lull, she left Mary and Bear at the shop and headed over to Between the Lines. Just as DeeDee had predicted, she'd devoured the first book in the Night series on Sunday, and now she needed a copy of the second book—the sooner the better.

As she stepped through the shop's screen door, she was surprised to see Emmet Baron emerging from the inner office, with a scowling DeeDee close behind. When he saw Kaylee, Emmet hesitated for just a moment, then gave her a curt nod and left, allowing the screen door to bang shut behind him. DeeDee started at the sound, but her expression softened when she noticed Kaylee.

Before her friend could say anything, Kaylee asked, "Emmet Baron?"

"Yes. I didn't realize you know him." DeeDee's scowl returned. "He was here to make me jump through a few more hoops even though the workshop is all set to go. It's not like he can back out now, of course, but that's not going to stop him from squeezing everything he can out of it." She shook her head. "It's a good thing I love the books so much."

Kaylee now realized why she'd recognized the name Puget Press the day before. "He's Griffin Graves's publisher, right?"

"Yes." DeeDee gave her a puzzled frown. "How exactly do you know him, anyway?"

Since DeeDee didn't have any customers, Kaylee moved toward her favorite chair. "I didn't until yesterday. He came into The Flower Patch trying to get me to sell some note cards."

DeeDee's face cleared. "Ah yes, the famous note cards." She gave a little laugh and gestured toward the counter. "I've got some right here. You know, under normal circumstances

I'd be happy to stock cards featuring the work of a local artist. But Emmet had to make it a condition of doing the workshop, even though the two things are completely unrelated. Nobody likes to do something under duress, even something they'd have otherwise done voluntarily."

"DeeDee," Kaylee said with concern, "I'm not sure Emmet Baron has the right to sell those cards."

Her friend looked up sharply. "Why do you say that?"

"When he told me that he owned the paintings, I asked him point-blank if he also controlled the reproduction rights."

"And?"

"Well, he said he did," Kaylee admitted, "but his behavior was very odd, and he all but ran out after that. I don't like to make accusations, but I have to tell you, I'm suspicious."

DeeDee sighed. "I didn't even think to ask him. Though when it comes to Emmet Baron, you're right to be suspicious. He has a terrible reputation: always pushing the boundaries, making his authors sign exploitative contracts, leaning on booksellers. And the fact that he's stumbled into such a hit with the Night books seems to have just made him worse. He uses that for leverage every chance he gets."

"How does he get away with it?"

"Well, that's the thing. Up until now, his behavior has mostly been a topic for shoptalk among booksellers in our region. But since the Night books have become such a hit, I suspect he's going to be under a lot more scrutiny. Let's hope, anyway." DeeDee began gathering up the boxes of note cards from the shop's counter. "Still, I'm going to put these away for now. I'll have to insist that he provide a written guarantee that he has the right to sell these, or I'll ship them right back to him." She paused, and then added with a smile, "But I think I'll wait until after the workshop for that."

Kaylee followed as DeeDee carried the note cards to the office. "I don't suppose that you'd let me borrow a set, would you?"

"Of course. But why on earth do you want them?"

Kaylee gave an embarrassed laugh. "Well, it's just . . . I can't seem to identify the plants in them."

"You, Kaylee Bleu, can't identify a plant? The world has turned upside down indeed."

Kaylee rolled her eyes at DeeDee's good-natured teasing. "Clive gave me a tour of the exhibit yesterday, and there were a number of these plant portraits. I really admired the detail and how easy it was to tell what each one was, even when the artist took a little creative license. But then when Baron brought these cards in yesterday, I didn't know what to think. It's the same level of detail, but I just couldn't tell what the plants were. It's been bothering me ever since."

"You could find a mystery under a rock in the middle of the desert," DeeDee said with a laugh, handing over one of the boxes. "Since you helped me out with the plants for the workshop, the least I can do is let you have one of these. That's why you came by, I assume? To check on the plants?"

"Actually, I came to get the next Night book," Kaylee confessed. "I'm sure the plants are fine, but we can definitely check on them too."

DeeDee gave her a distinctly self-satisfied grin, then led her to the corner of the store where the plants had been arranged to create a private nook for the workshop. Kaylee was about to comment on how well DeeDee had cared for them when she suddenly heard a commotion out in the street.

Both women froze, straining to listen. It sounded like two men having a heated argument, but Kaylee couldn't make out the words. After a few exchanges between the unseen men, DeeDee held up a finger to indicate one of the two voices and asked, "Isn't that Emmet?"

Kaylee had heard Baron's voice much less often than DeeDee, but she was inclined to agree. And then, as if to remove all doubt, the other voice suddenly became louder than ever, saying, "You're going to regret this, Emmet Baron. I swear you will."

Kaylee and DeeDee exchanged alarmed glances, then rushed to the bookstore's front door and gazed out into the street. But by the time they arrived, the only figure they could see was Emmet himself, hurrying away as quickly as his short legs could carry him.

4

After running home to drop off Bear and change from her work clothes into a summer dress, Kaylee returned to downtown Turtle Cove. Most of the town's street parking was full, so she parked in her usual spot at The Flower Patch and walked to the Randall Gallery for the opening. Dusk was already descending, so the lighted gallery at the far side of the business district stood out like a beacon. The sound of laughter and chatter from the guests floated on the warm summer air, growing louder as Kaylee approached. The event was in full swing, and people had even spilled outside.

Kaylee wondered for a moment if she would feel out of place. Through the large windows, she saw stylish people air-kissing and talking animatedly with one another, and she didn't immediately see anyone she knew. Maybe she would just say hello to Clive, check on her plants, and then quietly slip back out. She could head home to a quiet evening of reading on the porch with Bear at her feet.

It was warm inside with the press of people, and Kaylee had to stand on her tiptoes to look around. She nearly collided with a waiter bearing a platter of bite-size appetizers. "Sorry," she said.

"No worries," replied the waiter. "Clams casino? We also have smoked salmon crostini."

Kaylee was tempted, but she didn't want to find herself with a full mouth when she met up with Clive.

As if on cue, Clive appeared at her elbow and said, "Kaylee, what a pleasure!"

Kaylee took in Clive's tan linen suit and white shirt and

wondered if he'd dressed in neutrals so that he wouldn't clash with the art on the walls. "Thank you for inviting me. It's quite a turnout."

He nodded enthusiastically. "I can't thank you enough for the plants. They've really added to the presentation. In fact, I was wondering if you might be free to drop by tomorrow morning. I'd like to talk with you about keeping them longer than we'd agreed. Petra, Alexander!" He broke off to wave to a new couple just entering. "Petra, when am I going to get your work in here?"

While Clive was diverted by a tall, exotic woman in a black beaded cocktail dress, another waiter passed by with a platter of appetizers, and Kaylee took a mini baked brie. It smelled too good to resist.

"Now where was I?" Clive asked Kaylee, though his gaze continued flitting around the room. "Ah, you've found something to eat—good. There you are, Justine. Come meet Kaylee Bleu. She's responsible for the live plants here."

Kaylee quickly swallowed her hors d'oeuvre and smiled at the newcomer, a tall woman in her early thirties with straight, dark hair pulled back in a ponytail.

"Kaylee, this is Justine Lucas, Shirley Lucas's granddaughter." After the brief introduction, Clive immediately turned his attention to another guest. "Cassandra, darling, I love your new haircut," he said as he left Kaylee and Justine to chat.

Justine extended a hand to Kaylee. "I'm pleased to meet you," she said warmly. "I believe we have a mutual friend, DeeDee Wilcox. I visit her bookstore every time I come over to the island." Kaylee smiled at the connection, but before she said anything, Justine continued, "Clive said you'd had some insightful comments about Shirley's work."

"I don't know about insightful. I loved the paintings in the back room—"

"Shirley's portrait phase." Justine nodded with approval. "Not everyone gets those."

"I wasn't sure that I did at first." Kaylee noticed Justine straining to hear her, so she raised her voice to be heard above the din. "The works in this front room weren't all hung yet when I was here, so I didn't get a chance to see many of them."

"Let's elbow our way to the wall, then." Justine ducked into the crowd and Kaylee followed her toward the back wall. Traversing the packed room could have been slow going, but tall, graceful, self-assured Justine slipped easily between the partygoers, creating a path for Kaylee.

When they made it to the side wall, Kaylee caught a whiff of something she'd never expected to smell at a fine art gallery. "Is that barbecued pork?"

Justine nodded. "My brother, Darren, is doing a hog roast out back. I hope you're hungry. He'll make us a decent sandwich."

"It smells amazing," Kaylee said.

"Darren is trying to get a business going with our family recipe, so we asked Clive if we could set up the spit for the event tonight. I don't think it was exactly what Clive had in mind for the retrospective opening, but he agreed quite graciously when we proposed doing it."

"He certainly seems like a gracious person," Kaylee agreed, then gestured toward the closest painting. "So what can you tell me about this?"

"That's the first of what Shirley called her Herbaria series. She named it *Tangled Roots*, and it's actually a map of her herb garden, laid out in a maze pattern. Shirley imagined what it must look like underground."

Kaylee peered closer to admire the detail of the roots, translucent and meandering, as if drifting in water. Then she stepped back to take in the overall movement of the painting. "Fascinating.

I feel like I could get lost in it."

"Then you'll appreciate the next one, *Alice in the Herbarium.*" Justine shuffled a few feet to the left.

This artwork, Kaylee saw, was a painting of the cosmos—the sun, moon, stars, and planets—encapsulated in a glass terrarium. A child's curious face was just visible beyond the terrarium, distorted by the glass. The face wasn't noticeable immediately because the light emanating from the universe caught the eye first.

"I was actually the model for this one," Justine explained with a small smile. "I was ten. I couldn't sit still long enough for her to paint my picture. Finally she took a photo with a camera and used that as her reference."

"It's so charming," Kaylee said, "but like all of her paintings in this exhibit, the familiar things are somehow rendered so strange."

Justine nodded. They turned the corner to face two large paintings of identical size. Kaylee leaned close to read their labels. *Germi Nation* was an abstract explosion of color and lines, and *Blossoms in Decay* showed wildflowers growing from a compost pile.

"The detail in this one . . ." Kaylee found herself at a loss for words, and she clasped her hands behind her back to keep from reaching out to touch the painting.

"Not only that, but there's a poem running through the painting, like a thread." Justine ran her finger along the artwork without making contact. "You have to find the words in the heap."

"Wow," was all Kaylee could say as she examined the artwork.

Justine nudged Kaylee with her elbow. "Hey, I'm starved. Want to walk back and see if Darren will make us a sandwich?"

Kaylee's stomach grumbled. "That sounds wonderful."

She followed Justine's lead again, this time heading toward the hallway and the gallery's back door. As they navigated the room, Kaylee recognized a few people from the Turtle Cove business community, but in such a tight space, she didn't expect to capture anyone's attention unless they were right in front of her. Across a sea of heads, she saw Clive warmly greeting Nora Keller, the owner of Turtle Cove's other art gallery, Art Attack, and a talented painter in her own right. They appeared to be the very picture of friendly rivals.

As she approached the hallway, however, Kaylee noticed a sudden change in the room's vibe. Voices dropped a level. The couple standing nearest to her bent forward to whisper conspiratorially. Heads swiveled toward the entry, and then swiftly turned back. A few guests wore unfriendly, borderline hostile expressions on their faces.

Curious as to what was causing the fuss, Kaylee stood on her tiptoes and surveyed the room. The brash publisher, Emmet Baron, had made his way into the gallery. He was laughing and backslapping people he knew and pumping hands with a few others. A waiter with a tray of appetizers paused by Emmet, and he took two cocktail sausages by their toothpick handles. He ate them both in one bite, then tossed the toothpicks into the moss at the base of one of Kaylee's tall Kentia palms.

Kaylee glanced around her and saw that Justine had made considerable progress through the crowd. She tried to move a little faster, but she had to switch directions once or twice to keep up. When she looked back toward the front of the gallery, she saw Emmet Baron, now alone, take another handful of appetizers off the tray of a passing server. It was then that she recalled something odd: Emmet Baron claimed that he was putting on the exhibit, but Clive hadn't mentioned him at all during their consultation about the plants. She didn't see any sign of Clive now and the smell of the roasted pork was calling to her, so she forged ahead, pushing her doubts to the back of her mind.

When she escaped the crush of people inside the gallery and emerged into the sandy lot behind the building, Kaylee took a deep breath of cool evening air. There were plenty of people out here as well, but at least they were able to spread out.

Kaylee joined Justine, who was accepting two heavily laden plates from a tall, hefty man standing near a pig roasting on a large grill outfitted with a spit. Justine nodded toward two folding chairs arranged facing the grill, indicating that Kaylee should take one.

"I hope you don't mind sitting out here." Justine handed Kaylee one of the plates, which held a pork sandwich, then reached into a cooler and got her a bottled water. She gestured with the bottle. "Darren, meet Kaylee. Kaylee, this is my *little* brother, Darren."

Darren Lucas was anything but little. His broad build made Kaylee think of a bear. He wore heavy insulated gloves and had grabbed a mop from a large stew pot. He gave her a big grin and said, "Hey," waving the mop by way of greeting before swabbing the pig with marinade.

"The marinade is my grandfather's recipe," Justine explained. "We finally wrested it from him, and now Darren is taking up the mantle of being the family hog roaster, and planning to start his own food truck."

Darren nodded in agreement as he cranked the spit to rotate the pig. He gave it another swab on the other side, then replaced the mop, took off his gloves, and picked up a large cleaver to cut off chunks of meat.

Kaylee took a bite of her sandwich and marveled at the taste. "This is heaven."

"Isn't it?" Justine asked. "My little brother is good for something."

Darren gave Kaylee a thumbs-up, then stuck his tongue out at his sister before returning to his task. When he'd piled enough in a metal pan set on a prep table, a waiter came out and portioned the meat onto small brioche buns for sliders, then placed the sandwiches onto platters for the servers.

Kaylee took a few more bites of her sandwich, followed by a drink of water. "Do you live on Orcas Island?" she asked Justine.

"No, but Darren does. He's a deckhand on one of the supply ships that service the fishing vessels. Normally, anyway. We both took some time off to help Clive with the retrospective." Justine paused to take a sip of water. "I'm a linguist. I teach at Northwest Indian College, but I'm on sabbatical this year."

"Working on a book?" Kaylee inquired, her interest piqued by a fellow academic's professional pursuits.

"Sort of. I'm working with a team of educators and other linguists to develop language acquisition models for the Wakashan language family. My specific area is the Makah language. Our parents grew up on the reservation near Neah Bay, but neither spoke Makah. My grandfather knows a little, but he was discouraged from speaking the language when he was a kid. So here we are, trying to reclaim it." She peered at Kaylee in the dim outdoor lighting. "Do I detect some Native ancestry in you?"

"Good eye," Kaylee said. "My father is Quinault. He has always regretted not knowing the language."

"Many do. That's why I'm so passionate about this project." Justine took another bite. "So, Clive tells me you were a professor once."

"I taught plant taxonomy at the University of Washington, but I got laid off and honestly a little burned out, so I bought my grandmother's flower shop and her house."

Justine whistled. "Talk about a change. Has it worked out for you, moving from the big city to a small town?"

Kaylee beamed. "I love it here and I always have. I used to visit my grandparents a lot, so I knew the area pretty well already. Now, it's truly home." Kaylee took the last bite of her sandwich, then collected their empty plates and bottles and found a garbage can. When she returned to her chair, she said, "Tell me more about your grandmother. I have to admit I've fallen in love with her art."

"I think you would have loved her too." Justine glowed with familial pride. "She was anything but grandmotherly, which is why she insisted on us calling her Shirley. She had an infectious laugh, and she would laugh at anything. She would wander the garden by herself and stop and talk to a particular plant, then she'd burst into laughter. She used to say some of the plants told her jokes."

Darren chuckled nearby. "She was lonely when she was a kid," he explained to Kaylee. "Her sisters were way older, so she said she only had the plants in her mother's garden as playmates. She always said that her paintings were her way of letting other people see her plant friends the way she did." Darren had carved up a considerable amount of the pork, but the waiters were returning with empty platters less frequently now. He walked away and began sealing up the rest of the meat in large containers.

"I understand there is a book coming out about your grandmother. Or at least a catalog of the show?" Kaylee gestured toward the interior of the gallery.

Justine frowned. "That's not really a done deal."

Before Kaylee could ask more, they were interrupted by Darren's call of "Hey!" He was trying to get Justine's attention by waving his mop over his head.

"Watch it!" Justine scolded. "You'll get marinade in your hair, then you'll stick to your pillow tonight." She flashed Kaylee a smile. "That actually happened once, but we were kids."

Darren ignored that remark. "I'm about ready to load up. Can you keep an eye on this stuff while I get my truck?"

Just then, Clive appeared at the back door. "There you are, Justine. Can I borrow you? The art critic from *The Seattle Times* would love to meet you."

"Me? Now?" Justine glanced from Clive to Darren.

"I'll stay and watch Darren's stuff," Kaylee offered.

"Thanks, you're a lifesaver." Justine hurried to meet Clive, then they both disappeared into the gallery while Darren left to get his truck.

All of the other guests had also gone back inside, so Kaylee found herself alone in the back lot. The chatter from indoors reached her ears across the silence, and she thought it sounded a little like the tree frogs behind her house.

Suddenly, a sharp voice pierced the air. It was Clive, and he didn't sound pleased.

Kaylee could only hear the gallery owner's side of the conversation. "You're causing a scene," he said. "You need to leave." And then, in an incredulous tone, he demanded, "How did you get here, then?" After a beat, he sighed. "Fine, I'll call a cab for you."

Angling her head toward the door to the gallery, Kaylee saw Clive and Emmet standing just within. She turned away, not wanting to be caught witnessing an unpleasant scene, and was glad to see Darren arriving in a rumbly, rusty truck.

The driver's side door opened with a squeak. "Thanks, I've got it now," Darren said as he hopped out of the cab. "I'll have to come back tomorrow for the grill. It's too hot to handle at the moment."

He set to work packing the leftover marinade and bins of meat into a large cooler. Kaylee helped by folding up the picnic chairs, which Darren loaded into the truck. Then, he rinsed the marinade mop under a spigot attached to the gallery building, shook it out, and wrapped the head in a clean plastic bag cinched with a rubber band.

"Does the mop ever come clean again?" Kaylee asked.

"Sure. I pressure-wash it, then soak it in soapy water for a while, then pressure wash it again. If it's not clean enough after all that, I just get a new mop." His eyes twinkled, and suddenly Kaylee was unsure whether he was serious. She decided to believe that he was.

Darren put the mop in the bed of the truck and closed the tailgate. He climbed into the cab and waved through the open window. "Thanks for your help. Have a good one."

"Good night," Kaylee said. "Nice meeting you."

After Darren had pulled away, Kaylee finally returned to the gallery, hoping to say goodbye to Clive. She'd stayed much longer than she'd expected, and the crowd had thinned somewhat. As she passed the back gallery, she saw Emmet Baron standing by himself in a corner, but Clive wasn't in the room. She walked toward the front gallery to check for the owner. As she scanned the room from the doorway, a hand grabbed her elbow, startling her. She whirled to find Jessica.

"Have you thought about wearing bells?" Kaylee asked her friend. "I about had a heart attack."

"No, I've never considered that. Subtlety isn't my forte," Jessica said with a shrug.

"How long have you been here? I was out back talking to the artist's grandchildren."

"Not long, and I can't stay. I just wanted to pop by to support Clive, but from the looks of it, he didn't need any more support."

"You should have seen it earlier. Sardines have more breathing room."

"While I'm here, why don't you show me around? Just the nickel tour. It was a busy day and I wouldn't mind getting off my feet." Jessica gestured toward her strappy sandals. "I'm starting to regret my decision to wear my fancy shoes."

"Nickel tour it is." Kaylee led Jessica around the front gallery and pointed out a few of the paintings she liked best.

Jessica nodded appreciatively and made an occasional comment. When they stopped at one large artwork depicting a geranium whose balls of purple blooms were clustered in a crystal ball, she squealed in delight. "This one is identical to Oliver!" Oliver was the treasured lavender geranium she kept on the counter at Death by Chocolate, and she was convinced that the state of his leaves and petals foretold the future—the droopier his leaves or the more petals he lost, the gloomier the omen.

Kaylee chuckled as she examined the tag. "It's called *Truth or Lavendare*. And you could bring it home for the bargain price of—"

"Don't even tell me," Jessica said with a sigh. "I think it's time to find Clive to say hello and then get home. Sadly without this painting in tow."

"I'll leave with you," Kaylee said. "Let's check for Clive in the back gallery."

Jessica followed Kaylee into the hallway, but Kaylee stopped short when she spotted Darren standing just inside the back door, towering over Emmet Baron. The considerably shorter publisher was shoving his finger at Darren's chest and seemed to be hectoring him, though Kaylee couldn't make out what he was saying. Darren's face was flushed and angry. Suddenly, he gave Emmet a shove that knocked him to the floor.

Kaylee gasped, and Darren's head shot up. He held eye contact with her for a moment, then he spun and stomped off. As she and Jessica rushed toward Emmet, Kaylee heard Darren's truck engine revving, followed by the squeal of his tires as he peeled out.

Kaylee and Jessica joined a handful of other guests helping Emmet get to his feet. He swayed a bit and steadied himself with one hand on the wall. "I'm fine, just fine," he said, appearing

dazed. "I'm fine," he repeated. "I'm just waiting for my cab."
After a moment, he mumbled, "I need some air," and then
staggered out the back door. Nobody followed, and the door
closed behind him.

The crowd dispersed. Kaylee continued to eye the back door for
a moment, then said to Jessica, "I think that might be a sign to go."

"You can say that again," Jessica agreed. She pointed into the
rear gallery. "Clive seems to be pretty tied up at the moment."

Kaylee peered into the room and saw that the gallery owner
was deep in conversation with Justine and a man she assumed
was the art critic he'd mentioned. "I believe that's an art critic
he's with, so we'd better not interrupt. Ready to go?"

"Very. After one more peek at that painting of Oliver's cousin."

Kaylee and Jessica made their way through the crowd. They
waved at a few people they knew, including Bert and Ingrid
Greenleaf and Kathy Fitz, the head librarian at the Orcas Island
Library, and then, after one more viewing of *Truth or Lavendare*,
they exited through the gallery's front door.

The strong and distinctive odor of car exhaust hit Kaylee's
nose, and she wondered if it was from Darren's truck, though she
didn't recall smelling it earlier. Had he come back for his grill? *But
he said that it wouldn't be cool enough to transport until tomorrow
morning.* What had brought the young man back to the gallery?

"What happened in there?" Jessica asked, breaking into
Kaylee's pondering. "I feel like there's got to be a backstory
or something."

"The younger man was Darren Lucas, Shirley Lucas's
grandson," Kaylee explained. "The other man was Emmet Baron.
You don't know him?"

"No, but I've heard about him from DeeDee. I expect I'll be
getting a visit about those note cards soon enough."

"Honestly, I hope not," Kaylee said. "I'm not entirely certain

Mr. Baron has the right to sell them."

"Seriously?" Jessica could never resist a good conspiracy theory.

"I probably shouldn't say anything else until I know more for sure," Kaylee said apologetically. "I don't have any proof, and I'm not sure what Shirley Lucas's grandchildren do or don't know."

"What could make a nice guy like Darren want to shove Emmet?" Jessica wondered.

"Who knows?" Kaylee replied. "Although, the more I hear about Emmet Baron, the more I'm convinced that there could be any number of people who'd have a good reason to give him a shove."

Early the next morning in The Flower Patch work area, Kaylee took great joy in describing Shirley Lucas's artwork to Mary while Bear napped nearby. "Shirley seemed to have a deep connection to the plant life around her, and she captured each plant's personality in their portraits."

Mary arched an amused eyebrow. "Personality?"

"You'd have to see it to understand, I think. It's almost uncanny. You think the plants are going to wander right off the canvas. But on the other hand, anywhere she painted people, their faces were distorted or partially hidden."

"Maybe my boss will give me a long break one of these days so I can pop by the gallery," Mary said with a wink. "For now, though, we'd better get these patriotic bouquets for the Tortoiseshell Hotel done."

"Smart thinking." Kaylee trimmed the stem of the cornflower in her hand, then added it to the arrangement she was working on.

"So how was the opening?" Mary asked as she tied a ribbon

dotted with tiny flags in a bow. "Were there a lot of people?"

"If the number of guests is any indication, the show was a success, though I don't know how many paintings were sold, if any. I believe someone from the press was there too." Kaylee paused as a thought hit her. "I hope he didn't . . ."

"What?"

"Well, there was a bit of a dustup at one point, just before I left. I hope that doesn't become the story."

"Now you're being mysterious. What happened?"

"It was an argument between the artist's grandson, Darren, who is a pretty big guy, and the publisher Emmet Baron."

"The guy with the note cards you told me about?"

Kaylee nodded. "Darren shoved Baron, then stormed out. That's all I know, really. Fortunately, it was near the end of the evening."

"And this is the same guy who's been giving DeeDee so much trouble?" Mary started on another bow.

"I gather many people find him difficult. When he arrived, nobody seemed particularly happy about it, though that didn't deter him." Kaylee paused as a new thought struck her. "Between the gallery show and DeeDee's workshop with his author, we might be seeing quite a bit of this guy in the near future." She lowered her voice. "It's not a very nice thing to say, but I hope we don't."

Mary laughed. "Well, you're one of the friendliest people I know, so if you say that, then he must be pretty bad." She gestured at the arrangements on the workbench in front of her. "I'm going to start loading these into your car."

Mary had just hefted a vase when they heard a knock on the front door. While Bear jumped up excitedly at the prospect of a newcomer, the women exchanged dismayed glances. The Flower Patch wasn't due to open for another two hours.

"Should we just ignore it?" Mary asked.

"No, I'd better go see who it is. I'll give you a hand with those in a minute." Kaylee and Bear went to the front door, where she was confused to see Deputy Robyn Garcia through the glass. She unlocked the door and opened it. "Good morning. What brings you by?"

Garcia gave her a rueful smile. "Good morning, Kaylee. Sorry to bother you so early, but I'm afraid I need to speak to you about a man named Emmet Baron."

"Because of those note cards?" Kaylee asked, surprised that such a matter would warrant the attention of the sheriff's department.

Puzzlement washed over Deputy Garcia's face, and then she frowned. "No. Because he's dead."

5

A few minutes later, Mary bustled back into the shop after carrying a load of floral arrangements out to Kaylee's SUV. "Who was at the door?" she asked Kaylee, who was sitting in a chair near the register. "Oh hi, Robyn. I didn't see you there." The two knew each other well thanks to Mary's many years as a sheriff's department dispatcher.

"Good morning, Mary," the deputy said solemnly.

Mary's expression went from carefree to concerned. "What's the matter?"

"Emmet Baron," Kaylee said in a stunned voice. "After everything I was just saying, he's been murdered."

"Kaylee, that's not what I said. It's true that he had a superficial wound, but he was found facedown behind the gallery in soft, wet sand in such a way that his breathing would have been blocked," Robyn corrected her.

"How terrible," Mary said.

"We'll have to wait for the coroner's report, of course, but for the moment, the sheriff says there's no reason to think that this was anything more than what we call 'positional asphyxia.'" Garcia paused, then said, "He specifically told me to emphasize that we're not calling it murder, since we don't know exactly what happened yet."

Mary shook her head sadly. "Still, that's awful."

Instead of responding to Mary, Robyn gave Kaylee a quizzical look. "What did you mean just now when you said 'after everything I was just saying,' Kaylee?"

"I'd just been telling Mary about him." Kaylee's cheeks reddened and she grimaced. "I said I hoped we wouldn't be seeing too much of him."

Garcia pursed her lips, then switched gears. "Sheriff Maddox has asked me to talk with people who were at the reception last night. You were there, right?"

"Yes, but Mary wasn't," Kaylee replied.

The deputy pulled out a notepad and pen. "We understand that there was some sort of incident? Or incidents?"

"Yes, unfortunately," Kaylee said. "Incidents, plural."

"And from what you just said, it sounds like you knew Mr. Baron yourself?"

"That's putting it a little strongly. But yes, I'd met him. And his reputation preceded him."

Garcia started jotting down notes. "Kaylee, I need you to tell me everything you can remember about last night, including who else was there. So far, we only have a partial list."

"I'll tell you anything I know, of course," Kaylee said.

"That's what we're counting on. The sheriff sent me over here first because he says you have a good eye for this sort of thing."

Kaylee had used her background as a forensic botanist to help the sheriff's department solve a few crimes since moving to Turtle Cove, and the compliment filled her with pride.

"I'd appreciate it if you could also tell me whatever else you know or have heard about Mr. Baron."

When Kaylee glanced at the clock, Mary quickly said, "I can handle the delivery. Don't worry about it."

Kaylee smiled her thanks and handed over her car keys. Then she took a deep breath as she organized her thoughts. She had a lot to tell the deputy.

When Mary returned a little while before opening time, Deputy Garcia had just left and Kaylee was cleaning up the work area while Bear followed her around. The dog ran to greet Mary when she appeared, and she leaned down to give him an affectionate scratch behind the ears.

"He's happy to see you," Kaylee said.

"The feeling is mutual." Mary straightened and flashed a smile. "The folks at the Tortoiseshell were very pleased with our work. How did it go with Robyn?"

"As well as can be expected, I suppose," Kaylee said. "I told her everything I saw last night and about the note cards Emmet was trying to sell."

"What did she say?"

"Nothing, really. She just thanked me and left." Kaylee sighed and caught sight of the time. "I have an appointment with Clive Randall in half an hour. Do you think I should still go, even after what happened to Emmet Baron?"

"It's your call, but if it were me, I'd go."

"You're right. If it's not a good time, he'll tell me. Do you mind if I leave Bear here?"

"Of course not."

"Thanks. And I think I'd better leave now so I can stop and let DeeDee know what's going on." Kaylee washed her hands and ran her fingers through her hair to straighten it. "Be good, Bear," she called as she sailed out the door.

When Deputy Garcia had asked Kaylee if she knew of anyone else who might have any insight into Emmet Baron's business dealings, Kaylee had mentioned DeeDee's concerns about the publisher. Obviously there was no way DeeDee was involved in the man's death, but Kaylee knew that the police would be paying her a visit soon, and she felt she should give her friend notice that they'd be coming by. A cold sensation washed over

Kaylee when she realized that the publisher's death could interfere with the bookstore's writing workshop. *I certainly hope not, for the sake of everyone involved.*

When Kaylee crossed the street, she saw DeeDee through the store window, rearranging a display of the Books of the Night near the area reserved for the workshop. DeeDee must have sensed someone was watching her because she looked up sharply, then relaxed and smiled when she recognized Kaylee.

"Sorry to disturb you before opening, but it's serious," Kaylee said as DeeDee ushered her in and locked the door behind her. "Have you heard about Emmet Baron?"

"What about him?" DeeDee asked.

Kaylee swallowed hard. "He was found dead this morning behind Clive's gallery."

DeeDee gasped and collapsed in one of the easy chairs in the true crime section. Kaylee watched her as she processed the news.

"Dead?" DeeDee's words were tinged with shock. After a moment, she met Kaylee's gaze. "What happened? Did he—" She was interrupted by the whistle of the teakettle, and she stood. "Come to the back for a cup of tea and tell me what you know."

DeeDee led the way to her office, where she switched off the electric kettle. She pulled down two mugs from a shelf and filled them with steaming water. She handed an assortment of tea bags in a small wicker basket to Kaylee.

Kaylee thumbed through the contents while she spoke, but she didn't really see them. "Robyn Garcia came by the shop early. She's interviewing people who were at the party last night. From what she told me, Emmet was found by the garbage collectors this morning. He fell facedown and suffocated."

When Kaylee didn't continue, DeeDee asked, "Just fell?"

Kaylee shrugged. "That's what's brought out the sheriff's department. He had a bloody gash at the base of his head."

"So, is it murder?"

"The sheriff isn't calling it that—yet." Kaylee chose a chamomile tea bag and dunked it in her mug. "But I wanted to let you know that they'll probably want to interview you too. I told Robyn about your frustrations with Baron over the workshop and the things you've heard about him."

She spoke in an apologetic tone, but DeeDee was unperturbed. "To be honest, some of the stuff I told you is little better than rumor. I think I can point them in the right direction, though, at least for information about Emmet's dealings with local booksellers."

Kaylee sipped her tea, and she was a little surprised to find herself feeling calmer. "What about the workshop? Will it need to be canceled?"

DeeDee's brow furrowed, but she shook her head. "I don't see why. The arrangements are all made, the participants are all registered, and most of them are already in town. Andy and I picked up Griffin last night from the ferry and took him directly to Moira's place. I expect he's having coffee right now on the deck, watching the ocean." DeeDee leaned forward and rested her chin in her hand. "He may be upset when he finds out, though. He seemed a sensitive kid—er, young man."

"I wonder what this will mean for his publishing contract with Puget Press," Kaylee said. "Didn't you tell me that there's a ten-book series planned?"

"And Emmet Baron controlled everything."

"Really?"

"I'd bet money on it. Emmet preyed on inexperienced writers and had them sign over all rights. I've talked with some who regretted that decision." DeeDee took a sip of her tea. "To be fair, most of the books he publishes are one-offs, and many are second-rate. Most of those authors probably would have ended up self-publishing if not for him."

"But it sounds like Griffin is a different story."

"Griffin just happened to be that one in a million with an original mind, a fully imagined world, and a gorgeous prose style. The story is that he picked Puget Press because it was local and accepted unsolicited manuscripts. And Emmet took advantage of his innocence and lack of an agent. Signed him to a contract for a ten-book series, all rights."

Kaylee considered this. "Including adaptation rights? Didn't Jessica say there's a television series in the works?"

"Emmet held the keys to it all, right down to the merchandising," DeeDee said, gesturing at a display of dragon figures on her desk. "Many of Griffin's fans, including booksellers I know, are very resentful on his behalf."

"Oh, these are from the series!" Kaylee cried. "These are the dragons from Ellaryn, the world with all the plant life." She picked one up and examined it more closely. Catching sight of the price, she added, "Costs a bit much for a plastic toy."

DeeDee shrugged. "Emmet described them as a limited edition. You're right, they don't look like much, but you should see what they go for online. And you're right about the TV series too, at least if the Internet is to be believed. They say there will be a big announcement soon. But the word is that Griffin won't get a penny from any of it." She sighed. "That's what people are saying, anyway. I don't know the actual details of his contract. I do know that that's why writers should always have an agent, though."

"I can imagine him feeling trapped by that." Kaylee swirled the dregs of her tea as she wondered whether Griffin could secure release from the contract now, or at least renegotiate it. Then a clock somewhere in the shop chimed, bringing her out of her reverie. "Sorry, DeeDee, I've got to keep my appointment with Clive at his gallery."

"Heading over to the scene of the crime, are you?"

Kaylee felt a knot in her stomach tighten at the idea that Emmet's cause of death was anything but an accident. "I certainly hope not."

6

A couple of sheriff's cruisers were parked in front of the gallery when Kaylee arrived, but she assumed the real activity was out back. She peered down the alley to the sandy lot as she passed and saw that there was yellow caution tape across the far end. The front door was locked, but through the picture windows she could see Clive pacing nervously and speaking to someone on his cell phone. Once he hung up, she tapped on the window to get his attention.

"We're closed!" he called without facing her.

Kaylee tapped again. Clive turned around with annoyance, but when he saw her, he readily let her in.

"I'm sorry I was so rude," Clive said apologetically. "It's been quite a morning."

"I can imagine," she replied.

"We're to stay in the front gallery only." He escorted Kaylee to a couple of contemporary chairs that had been set up in the center of the room. Once she took a seat, Clive sat down and pressed his hands together as if in prayer. "This can't be happening. And on the day after the opening!"

"I'm so sorry about all this, Clive," Kaylee said sympathetically. She heard the squawk of a police radio in another room and assumed there were a few deputies inside the building with them.

Clive waved toward the sounds. "They've turned the place inside out. They're out in force interviewing everyone who was at the party. It seems that they've heard all about my argument with Emmet, not to mention his little spat with Darren. They even searched my car and my briefcase. And they say they're going to search my house."

"I think they need a warrant for that," Kaylee said in an attempt to console him.

"I gave them permission. Doing anything else would just make me look bad." He trained frightened eyes on her. "Kaylee, I think they consider me a suspect."

Kaylee refrained from stating that this did not seem unreasonable to her, given that Emmet had been found on his property. Instead, she said, "A suspect for what? My understanding is that they are treating this as an accident or a natural death of some sort."

"That's what they're saying for now, but they told me that someone probably hit him on the head." He shuddered. "How long before they decide it's a murder?"

"I have faith in the police," Kaylee said. "They're methodical and careful. They'll discover the truth, no matter what it is."

"I hope you're right. They're in my framing room now, moving things around as if they have bear paws instead of hands." Clive sighed with resignation. "Well, if it is murder, I can take comfort in the fact that I won't be the only suspect. There was no shortage of people who wanted Emmet dead."

Kaylee gazed at him quizzically. "What makes you say that?"

"If you'd known him even a little, you'd get what I mean." Clive shook his head. "For instance, what kind of man can come to a party that he isn't even throwing and manage to get into two altercations? It's a rare talent."

Kaylee considered Clive's "isn't even throwing" comment. "I didn't really know Emmet, but he did say something to me about this exhibit. In fact, he implied that he was at least partly responsible for it."

"Patently untrue," Clive said crisply, "but so like Emmet to try to take credit."

"So you knew him well?"

"We moved in some of the same circles for years. He fancied himself a supporter of the arts, both literary and visual. You know he was a publisher, right? Whenever anything cultural was in the works on Orcas Island, we would often both find ourselves involved." He gestured at the walls of his gallery. "And then more recently there was this."

"You mean the exhibit?"

"Not specifically. I think I told you that I have been representing Shirley Lucas's work ever since she and I were both starting out. She got into painting later in life, you see." Kaylee nodded and he continued. "Well, a year or so ago, Emmet got the idea that he wanted to collect Shirley's work. I recently sold him a number of her paintings." He gestured again. "Some of them are part of this exhibit."

"What got him interested in Shirley Lucas?"

"Not aesthetic sense, I'm sure," Clive said haughtily. "It was about the time that interest in her work really started to take off, and since she was local, I think Emmet just saw a chance to get in on the ground floor."

"And he loaned some of them back for this exhibit?"

"And even in that he had to be difficult, of course."

"How so?"

"He wouldn't loan the *Orcas Island Triptych*." At Kaylee's puzzled expression, he explained, "It was Shirley's last completed work before she died. A painting done in three panels like nothing you've ever seen. Emmet bought it in a private sale that I arranged. As her last work, it would have provided the perfect capstone for the exhibit, but he flat-out refused."

"Why would he do that?" Kaylee asked. "Especially when he had loaned others?"

Clive shrugged. "I never could get an explanation out of him. He just adopted a mysterious tone and said that he had 'special plans' for it." He put air quotes around the words and said them with a hint of disgust. "The grandchildren have expressed interest in buying it back for sentimental reasons. It's possible that withholding it from the exhibit was a strategy to jack up the price. I don't know."

"That sounds pretty mercenary."

"That was Emmet to the core. He lived beyond his means, went through money like it was water. Bought this expensive house up on Mount Constitution—there was an article about it in one of the local lifestyle magazines that generated quite a bit of buzz at the time, although he probably whipped up all that buzz himself. I think he believed that looking rich and acting rich would attract more money, better business prospects. But it was just a lot of smoke and mirrors."

"You said he was a publisher?" Kaylee prompted, interested to see how Clive's perspective would compare with DeeDee's.

"That he was." Clive sat back in his chair and crossed his arms. "Years ago, he bought a struggling publishing house very cheaply. That was how he got his start, and I gather he did make a go of it. He put out a lot of travel books, local history, books on Native American lore—the things tourists buy. I don't know much about the business, but my understanding is that publishing has pretty low margins at the best of times."

"Speaking of the best of times," Kaylee said, "I understand he's done quite well with these Griffin Graves books."

"Ah, the young savior. That was a winning roll of the dice for sure. Rather a surprise to Emmet, I think, though he quickly reached the point where he wouldn't admit his luck. It was during the first flush of that success that he bought the triptych. Still, success only reinforced all his worst instincts. I think he expected a payday of even greater magnitude when Hollywood came calling—and he didn't hesitate to live today on the basis of tomorrow's expectation." Clive brooded in silence for a moment, then added, "Still, they are wonderful books. Have you read them?"

Kaylee smiled. "My friends talked me into it, and now that I've started, I can't get enough."

"I'm right there with you. And I'm neither a mystery buff nor a fantasy fan."

"Any interest in his workshop at Between the Lines?"

Clive laughed and shook his head. "I'm a visual person, not a writer. But I will definitely attend his reading."

They sat for a while in silence, then Clive said, "I'm sorry. I know I asked you here to consult further about Shirley's work, but with all this going on . . ." He gestured vaguely.

"Of course," Kaylee said. "Though I'd be happy to reschedule to another time if you're still interested."

"Thanks. I'll be in touch."

As she rose to leave, Sheriff Eddie Maddox appeared from the back of the gallery. "Kaylee," he said, "I thought I heard your voice. Clive here has told me about the incident last night between Emmet Baron and Darren Lucas, but Robyn tells me that you were a witness to that as well."

It was a statement rather than a question, but Kaylee nodded confirmation anyway.

"I was wondering if you'd come back here and tell me about it in as much detail as you can remember," the sheriff said.

Clive appeared about to rise and join them, but Maddox stopped him. "If you'll excuse us, Mr. Randall."

After giving a curt nod, the gallery owner remained in the front room while Kaylee followed the sheriff into the hallway.

"Okay, Kaylee," Sheriff Maddox said. "Can you show me where the altercation occurred?"

"Sure," Kaylee said, walking to the spot where the two men

had faced off the night before. "Emmet was standing here, and he was shoving his finger in Darren's chest. He was angry, but there was so much noise from the gallery that I couldn't hear what he was saying. He seemed to be the one doing all the talking, and then Darren seemed to have had enough. He knocked Emmet's arm away and shoved him. Emmet fell, and Darren left. I heard his truck peel out."

"Then what did you do?"

"A few people nearby were trying to help Emmet up, and Jessica and I joined them. He was pretty unsteady, but he didn't say a word about what had happened. He just said he was fine and was waiting for a taxi. Then he went out to get some air." She gestured toward the back door.

"Randall claims he called for a taxi, but we haven't been able to track it down yet." He peered at Kaylee. "Did you see Baron get in a taxi? See which way he went?"

Kaylee shook her head. "Jessica and I left from the front door. I didn't see him outside, but he'd gone out the back way, and he could have been back there still."

Maddox's phone rang, and he excused himself to answer it. He stepped a few paces away and listened intently for some time. Kaylee didn't intend to eavesdrop, but when she heard him ask, "Anyone hurt?" she couldn't help but be curious. There was a lengthy pause before Maddox asked, "And you're back now? You've got him there?" The conversation finally concluded with the sheriff saying, "No, you did the right thing. Keep him there for now. I'll be there as soon as I can."

Putting the phone back in his pocket, Maddox sighed and then returned his attention to Kaylee. Tilting his head in the direction of the front room, he said, "I would also like to hear your account of the other incident last night."

Kaylee shook her head. "I wasn't much of a witness for that

one, I'm afraid. I was out back by the grill with Darren Lucas. I heard a commotion inside, which sounded to me like Clive yelling at Emmet Baron. Or not yelling, maybe, but . . . I suppose a good word might be remonstrating. He was accusing Baron of causing a scene, and he told him that he should leave." She thought for a moment. "For what it's worth, I did hear Clive say that he was going to call Emmet a cab."

"Since you were out back during the party, would you mind checking it out with me? You may have seen something important and not realize it."

"Sure," Kaylee said. "But it was pretty dark, and I spent most of the time talking to Justine Lucas."

When they exited through the back door, Kaylee immediately noticed a patch of sandy earth that had been demarcated with yellow police tape tied to stakes planted in the ground. Darren's grill sat in the same spot as last night, not far from the cordoned-off area. Apparently he had never returned to pick it up.

While the sheriff jotted down notes, Kaylee did her best to recall anything she'd seen in the lot the night before. She described the cars she'd seen, including Darren's rumbly old pickup and the van emblazoned with the caterer's name and phone number. After she'd exhausted her memory, they went back into the gallery.

As they stepped through the back door into the hallway, Kaylee heard a commotion from the front gallery. Hurrying down the hall, they found Clive rapidly backing away from a distraught Justine Lucas.

"Tell me where he is!" Justine demanded. "They told me that he's here." As soon as Maddox and Kaylee entered the room, Justine rounded on them, eyes flashing. "Sheriff, why have you arrested my brother?"

7

Justine was clearly upset, but she also appeared to be doing her best to keep herself under control. "Darren didn't kill Emmet Baron," she said in a strained voice, and Kaylee wondered if she heard a note of doubt along with all of the other emotions.

"Miss Lucas," the sheriff said in a calm and measured voice. "Your brother hasn't been charged with anything, and certainly not murder."

Kaylee saw relief flood Justine's face.

"However," Maddox continued, "he is in custody. He was belligerent with my officers when they went to question him this morning. And he was getting ready to board the ferry to the mainland despite being warned not to."

"But he was just going to get our grandfather," Justine protested. "He's supposed to bring him over to the island today."

Maddox shook his head. "I'm sorry, Miss Lucas, but I'm going to have to ask that this take priority. I realize it's an inconvenience, and I apologize. But we have an unexplained death, and that's a serious matter."

"Yes, but—" Justine tried to interject, but the sheriff held up a hand.

"Your brother was seen by multiple witnesses having words with the deceased shortly before he died. I need to have a conversation with him before we can decide what the appropriate next steps are. Do you understand?" Though his words were unyielding, his tone was sympathetic.

The fight seemed to drain out of Justine, and she stood

chewing her lip for a moment before giving a reluctant nod. "I can go pick up my grandfather later in the week. Can I see Darren?"

"You're welcome to come down to the station and wait, but you can't see him until after I've talked with him."

Justine gave a rueful smile. "Truth is, he'd get mad if I came down."

"You're welcome to wait here if you'd like, Justine," Clive said.

"Actually" —Justine swiveled her gaze to Kaylee— "I wonder if I could have a few minutes of your time?"

Kaylee was surprised at the request, but she nodded. Then she frowned, remembering that Mary was alone at The Flower Patch. "Would you mind coming back to my shop with me? I've been gone for a while and I need to check in."

"Sure," Justine said. "Why don't I meet you there in twenty minutes? I need to call my grandfather to let him know what's going on."

Kaylee agreed and gave Justine directions, then said goodbye to the sheriff and Clive and walked back to the shop.

A short while later, the front door of The Flower Patch chimed with Justine's entrance, and Bear trotted over to greet her. "Hello there, little guy," she cooed, squatting down to let him sniff her hand, then rubbing his ears.

"That's Bear," Kaylee said approaching from the front counter. "He's our resident greeter."

"He's a cutie. How many bow ties does he have?"

Kaylee blushed. "More than is reasonable. I think his wardrobe is bigger than mine at this point, but I can't help myself."

Justine laughed. "Ah, the things we do for our pets."

Mary had agreed to keep an ear out for the door chime while she worked on an impressive birthday bouquet, so Kaylee led Justine to the sitting room she used for consultations.

When both women were settled in the room's comfortable

chairs, Kaylee said, "I'm sorry if Darren is in any trouble. I quite enjoyed meeting him."

A series of emotions raced across Justine's face, from worry to exasperation. Finally, she said, "Darren and trouble are not exactly strangers. But I truly don't believe he has it in him to kill anyone."

"I don't think the police believe that anyone *killed* Emmet, necessarily." At a questioning look from Justine, Kaylee explained the possibility of positional asphyxia.

"Well, the sheriff might have told me that," Justine said bitterly. "And I suppose he'll keep that from Darren as well to try and trip him up."

Kaylee didn't want to speculate about how Eddie Maddox might conduct his interrogation, so instead she said, "I believe that they're talking to everyone who was there last night."

"Sure, but as soon as they heard about Darren, they went straight for him, didn't they?"

Again, Kaylee avoided commenting on the police's conduct. "Do you have any idea what the disagreement was about?"

For a moment, Justine scowled, then she laughed. "So it's true, then." She paused to study Kaylee. "I told you last night that I know DeeDee. And she's told me a little about her friend Kaylee Bleu, the police consultant who solves murders. When I saw you this morning, I thought maybe a police consultant was just what Darren and I need."

Kaylee got the sense that Justine was more worried about her brother than she was letting on. "I'd be happy to help in any way I can, but as we were just saying, we're not even sure the police will conclude that it's murder."

Justine issued a derisive snort. "Emmet Baron? My money's on murder."

"What makes you say that?"

"The man was a snake." Bitterness edged Justine's words. "Greedy, unscrupulous, conniving. He seemed to think that because he had bought a few of my grandmother's paintings that he had some sort of proprietorial interest in her entire life's work."

"Are you referring to the book of your grandmother's work?"

"There is no book," Justine said heatedly. "Although the notion of it has eaten up months of our lives. Are you familiar with copyright issues pertaining to paintings?"

"I've heard a little bit, but not much."

"Well, I've had to become an expert, and the basic point is that just because you buy a painting, it doesn't mean you can do whatever you like with it. You can display it, and you can sell it, but you can't reproduce it to make money off of it. Like by putting it in, say, a book."

Kaylee nodded her understanding. "But surely that's pretty straightforward. Wouldn't Emmet have known that?"

"Oh he knew, I'm sure," Justine said. "But he was trying to get it done behind our backs. I think he was hoping that if the book was a *fait accompli*, we wouldn't do anything about it. So he'd been going around to people who own Shirley's work, pretending it was all aboveboard and getting their permission to use their paintings. We didn't know a thing about it until a few months ago, when one of the owners asked us in all innocence how the book was going."

"That must have been quite a shock."

"Oh it was. Fortunately, we jumped on it right away. We contacted everyone he had talked to and explained the situation, asking them to withdraw their permission. Many of them did, but I think he might have gone ahead anyway if we hadn't also gotten a lawyer and served him with an injunction." Justine shook her head. "I don't know what he was thinking at that point."

"Did he dispute that you and Darren control the rights?" Kaylee asked.

"That was his argument. He claimed that my grandmother's death meant that the owners of the works now controlled full copyright. But it's just not the case. The law is clear that the copyright stays with the artist's estate, and Darren and I are the heirs of that estate. Emmet kept saying he'd continue to fight it."

"How could he fight it? The law seems clear."

"He turned really nasty and kept threatening us with lawsuits. Even though he has no legal grounds, just the threat is enough. It would cost a lot of money to go to court to defend ourselves, and he knew it. It's made our lives hell." Justine gazed down at her lap. "I probably shouldn't be saying all this. It makes us look bad."

Kaylee shook her head. "You should be as up-front as possible. My experience with criminal investigations is that things like this always come out eventually. It's trying to hide them that makes people seem guilty. Besides, you've already got a lawyer who can vouch for all this."

Justine nodded and seemed to take some comfort from the thought.

Not wanting to rob Justine of her moment of relief, Kaylee hesitated to bring up the note cards. However, she knew that the other woman needed to know about all of Emmet's schemes regarding Shirley Lucas. "Excuse me for a moment." Kaylee went upstairs to the flower shop's office and retrieved the set of cards she'd gotten from DeeDee. When she returned to the sitting room, she held out the stack to Justine. "Have you seen these?"

As Justine accepted the note cards and examined them, her face clouded over. "This is the *Orcas Island Triptych*!" She angrily spread the cards out on the table. "Where did you get these?"

"Emmet Baron was going around to local businesses trying to get them to stock them."

"And you agreed?" Justine asked sharply.

"He came here, but I said no. As I told you, I've heard a little about reproduction rights issues. I actually asked him if he controlled the rights for these."

"What did he say?"

"He claimed that he did, but he left right after that, which I found suspicious. He insisted that DeeDee put some on display as a condition of hosting the Griffin Graves workshop." Kaylee couldn't tell if Justine recognized the name or not. "But I can assure you that DeeDee does not have them out for sale."

"If anybody did sell the note cards, the money belongs to Shirley's estate." Justine groaned. "Now we're going to have to find out who else in town has them."

"If I can help, let me know," Kaylee offered.

Justine shook her head, her mind clearly racing. "This is just like Emmet. He was such a rat!" Her words dripped with vitriol. "He's even making our lives miserable from beyond the grave."

Kaylee took note of the raw emotion in Justine's voice. She liked the woman, and very much wanted to trust her—but she was also quite sure that she wouldn't want to get on her bad side.

8

Traffic in The Flower Patch the rest of the day was so heavy that Kaylee didn't even have time for a lunch break. She heard a lot of excited chatter about the body that was found, but no one seemed to know the victim—or much care who he was, which saddened Kaylee quite a bit. *Imagine having your whole life reduced to morbid gossip.*

When she finally got home that evening, Kaylee sat in her SUV for a few minutes, taking in the undulating pinks and purples of the lavender fields in the waning daylight. She nervously tapped her fingers on the steering wheel as she reviewed everything that had happened during the last twenty-four hours. Her mind churned in circles with images of Emmet, Clive, Darren, and Justine.

As if sensing she needed comfort, Bear climbed into her lap and licked her chin. Running her fingers along his back did indeed have a soothing effect, and after a few moments Kaylee felt settled enough to head inside for the night. She couldn't wait to kick off her shoes and relax.

Unfortunately, her peace of mind didn't last for long. As she was unlocking the door, the phone in the kitchen started to ring. She managed to grab it just before it went to voice mail.

"Kaylee, it's Eddie." The sheriff's voice was calm and steady, but even so, Kaylee's heart started to race at the thought of what he might want at this hour.

"What's up?"

"I'd appreciate your help with a little matter. We found something today at Emmet Baron's house that we could use your expertise on. Would you be able to meet me there tomorrow morning, say ten o'clock?"

It sounded like a request, but Kaylee knew it wasn't. "Of course, anything I can do. Can you give me an idea of the issue?"

"It's plant related, as you might have guessed, but maybe a little complex to go over on the phone. We'll all have clearer heads in the morning." He gave her detailed directions to Emmet's house and then said good night.

As she set the phone back in the receiver, Kaylee sighed and leaned against the counter. *So much for relaxing tonight.*

After a fitful night of sleep, Kaylee set out for Emmet Baron's house, which was situated near the top of Mount Constitution. The road up the mountain had been dramatic, cutting through a national forest with many curves. Kaylee had caught glimpses of the ocean through the Douglas fir trees that canopied over the narrow road. But when she'd reached a clearing and her GPS told her she'd arrived at her destination, she had found a modest, brick ranch house that didn't seem to do justice to its setting.

She climbed out of her red Ford Escape and said good morning to the sheriff, who was standing beside his cruiser. Next to the cruiser was an older model Honda Civic, which she eyed curiously as a pudgy man emerged clutching a briefcase.

"Morning, Mr. Putnam." Nodding toward the stranger, Eddie explained, "Kaylee, this is Albert Putnam. Since we haven't been able to locate any kin, we asked the judge to expedite appointing a representative for the estate. Mr. Putnam is an attorney from Seattle who has occasionally represented the interests of Puget Press."

The attorney's dark hair was combed over to disguise a balding pate. He wore brown pants and a short-sleeved ecru shirt with a brown tie. "Nice to meet you," he said politely.

"Likewise," Kaylee said. "I'm Kaylee Bleu."

"Kaylee is the plant taxonomist I mentioned yesterday," the sheriff said. "She consults with us occasionally on matters relating to plants."

"So what are we doing here?" Kaylee asked.

"Let's go inside and I'll explain." The sheriff pulled out a set of keys, and Kaylee realized with a jolt that they probably had been Emmet's.

As they approached the ranch, a second look proved no more impressive than the first. The house clung to the mountainside, facing the ocean. A wide chimney cut the terra-cotta roof in half, and the only windows facing the road were small and high up.

Inside, the house belied its modest exterior, and Kaylee began to understand the excitement generated by the article Clive had mentioned. The side walls were mostly glass, with a skydiver's view of air and ocean. The flooring throughout was rustic blue terra-cotta tile. A few steps down led to an open living room, whose dizzying exposure was anchored by an extra-large yellow brick fireplace, flanked by floor-to-ceiling bookcases. Three oversize, cloud-like sheepskin rugs dotted the floor.

"I feel like I'm floating in here," Kaylee said, marveling at the opulence of the house. As she took it all in, she realized that there wasn't a plant in sight. It wasn't unusual for a second home, but it made her wonder exactly what she was doing there. She voiced as much. "I don't see any plants, Sheriff. What is it that you need me for?"

Instead of Maddox, it was Mr. Putnam who answered. "As I was searching for a will or other paperwork, I found some letters that refer to rare plants." He paused as if wondering what to say next, and Kaylee became more puzzled than ever.

"Why don't we start with a tour?" Maddox suggested.

Kaylee followed the sheriff and Mr. Putnam as they circled the house. Art filled the walls, and shelves were lined with Native American artifacts and pottery. In Emmet's bedroom was a carved totem pole that served as a support beam.

"A number of totem poles were made in the 1930s as part of the Indian New Deal program and sold to tourists," Mr. Putnam explained. "He's lucky he got one that's been so well-preserved."

"Do you know a lot about Native history, Mr. Putnam?" Kaylee asked.

"Actually, there's a plaque on the side table there explaining the origin as well as the controversy over the cultural appropriation inherent in the program. These symbols that had been so important to Native American culture were merely fashionable to white people, and they lost a lot of their meaning when they were just made to be sold as decorations."

They left the bedroom and walked down a wide, galley-like hallway lined with more paintings. There were a couple of gaps, which Mr. Putnam explained were where two Shirley Lucas paintings had hung before they were loaned to the Randall Gallery.

"Then there is this," Albert said as they rounded a corner. "The *Orcas Island Triptych*."

Kaylee's breath caught in her throat. Larger than anything she had expected, the three paintings were unlike the others she'd seen in the gallery, yet they were unmistakably the work of Shirley Lucas. Emmet's note cards didn't even begin to do them justice.

The center panel was a portrait of a plant much in the style of the *Mona Lisa*, with a close rendering of the subject in front of a distant harbor view. At the bottom of the image, two of the plant's leaves lay one on top of the other, as if they were hands resting in a lap. Based on the fir trees framing the harbor, Kaylee recognized the East Sound. Painted along the edges was an elaborate gold filigree that was so detailed that Kaylee was tempted to reach out and touch it to make sure it wasn't part of the frame itself. The two outer panels depicted meadow scenes overflowing with smaller versions of the plant in the center panel. All of the flora was full of life and personality, and Kaylee couldn't help but smile.

"Is there any documentation or notes about the area she was painting?" she asked.

"Well, that's one of the questions," Mr. Putnam said uneasily. "Of course she may have given some interviews where she talks about the triptych. That would need to be dug up from archives unless the family kept copies."

"Kaylee, can you identify these plants?" the sheriff asked.

She stepped closer to the painting and gazed at the center panel. She was seized with the same combination of frustration and fascination that she'd felt when she had first seen the note cards. She studied the three panels for a long time, moving in close and then stepping back again, but the identity of the plants eluded her. Finally, she released a frustrated sigh. "No, I can't say offhand. May I take some pictures to compare to my reference books?"

"You may," Eddie said. "Though it appears the victim had already done so and had reprinted them as note cards."

Kaylee nodded. "I've seen them, and they're not particularly good likenesses." She pulled out her phone and systematically photographed the paintings, first from a distance, and then in sections. When she was finished, she joined the sheriff and Mr. Putnam, who had hung back while she worked. "If I may ask, what's the urgency about identifying the plants Shirley Lucas painted?"

Maddox and the attorney exchanged glances.

Mr. Putnam cleared his throat. "We found some correspondence in Emmet's desk addressed to three developers who are vying to build on the old Caslon tract."

Kaylee nodded, though she knew little about the deal except the name of the plot and that it was a high-profile project.

"Emmet seemed to think that Shirley had discovered a rare plant on that bit of land," the attorney continued.

"And that could stall development there, at least while research is underway," Kaylee concluded. "Did Emmet have a business interest in the parcel or the development proposals?"

"He wanted to," Mr. Putnam said.

"We're still establishing the facts," Maddox said. "At first glance, it appears that Emmet Baron was claiming that a plant otherwise thought to be extinct is growing on this specific parcel. He says in the letters that he has proof."

Kaylee felt her pulse quicken slightly. The discovery of a living example of an extinct species would be thrilling—as a botanist, it would be far more exhilarating for her than whatever development was planned for the land.

Eddie continued. "It appears that Baron was trying to leverage this claim to get in on the action. I'll have copies of the letters he wrote sent to you."

Kaylee thought for a moment. "So you're thinking this may be a motive for murder. Or at least for an attack."

Maddox and Albert answered Kaylee with silence. She ran her fingers through her hair while she pondered the possibility of Emmet's "discovery" being real.

"Such things do happen," she said at last. "There was a lot of excitement not too long ago among botanists about the discovery of a native plant thought to be extinct in Vermont. Maybe Emmet was onto something."

The sheriff smiled. "That's where you come in."

9

"The triptych is actually owned outright by Emmet—or now by his estate," Mr. Putnam noted as he and Kaylee started an inventory of the rest of the items in the house. It wasn't what Kaylee had been called in to do, but she saw that she could be of help, and frankly, her curiosity was getting the best of her. She called Mary and arranged for her to watch the shop for the rest of the morning. The attorney had Kaylee describe each item as thoroughly as possible while he entered the information into his laptop.

"How do you know that, Mr. Putnam?" Kaylee asked.

"Call me Albert, please," he said. Though he was unfailingly polite, his intonation remained flat. "And I found the receipt for the painting on top of his desk. Not in a file, but next to the letters to the developers. That may suggest that he was considering selling the paintings."

"Is that unusual?"

"Actually, yes. Many of these items seem to be here on loan," Albert explained. "I've also found quite a number of loan agreements. He did use this house for business purposes—publication parties and so forth—and so the claim would be that there was some value in having notable pieces displayed here. Those Inuit carvings on the shelves, for instance, as well as many of the paintings."

"Sounds like quite a nice arrangement for him," Kaylee said, glancing around with fresh eyes.

"'Nice' is one word," Albert said. "Emmet may have been taking advantage of the situation. It appears that he could have used these borrowed pieces as collateral for a personal loan."

Kaylee gaped at him. "But if he didn't own them, is that legal?" Albert shook his head. "There are a lot of legal tangles here."

That sounds like an understatement. "I imagine the borrowed art will be returned?"

"Eventually. For now, I'll continue the inventory, keep searching for a will, and, for the time being, meet his business obligations."

"It's a big job that you didn't ask for."

Albert's gaze remained on his laptop screen. "Well, it won't be the first time. Emmet Baron's business affairs were anything but boring."

Kaylee returned to The Flower Patch to find it packed with customers. Tourists and idle browsers made up much of the crowd, but there was also a steady stream of people preparing their floats for the upcoming Fourth of July parade. They all wanted to consult on appropriate floral accents for their displays.

Fortunately, things had slowed by that afternoon, when Deputy Garcia arrived with the photocopies of the letters that Sheriff Maddox had promised. Mary had just returned from a late lunch and Kaylee was about to take her own even later lunch, so the correspondence arrived at an opportune moment.

"Before you go," Kaylee said to the deputy, "you and the sheriff both mentioned the wound on Emmet's head."

Robyn nodded without comment.

"So somebody attacked him in some way, even if that wasn't the cause of death. And I told you how DeeDee and I heard someone threaten Baron in the street."

"The sheriff really wishes you knew who'd done that," Robyn said.

"So do I. My point is that Emmet Baron seems to have rubbed a lot of people the wrong way. Have you run across any previous incidents where someone attacked him?"

"You mean aside from Darren Lucas?"

"Something serious, I mean. Not just a shove. Something that could result in a wound like the one you found on the body."

Robyn hesitated. "We're really not supposed to discuss an open investigation, but I know that the sheriff has asked for your help. No, we haven't uncovered any previous incidents like that yet."

Yet? "He does not appear to have been a well-liked man," Kaylee observed. "Is the sheriff expecting to find something like that?"

"Your guess is as good as mine," Robyn said, then said goodbye and left Kaylee with the letters.

As she ate a quick lunch in the shop's kitchen, Kaylee read through the letters. They were all written by Emmet Baron, they were addressed to three different developers, and they all concerned the piece of land known as the Caslon tract. Real-estate development was outside her area of expertise, and the names meant little to her. She'd heard them mentioned or seen them in the newspaper, but she otherwise knew little about Roger Findley, Jim Park, or Hank Liebling.

In all three letters, Baron was ostensibly offering his services as an "environmental consultant." Kaylee knew that Baron had turned his hand to many things, but this was the first time she'd heard of him having any expertise in this area. Still, it was the wording of the letters that struck her.

It is imperative that you be aware of the suspected presence on the site of certain rare species of endangered or otherwise extinct plants. Their presence is attested to by the work of a local painter familiar with both plants and the site. If confirmed, the presence of these protected plants is certain to raise complications in—and perhaps permanently derail—the permitting process. Allow me to provide you with the guidance necessary to establish the truth about this possibility and ensure a smooth permitting process.

"If confirmed," Kaylee repeated to herself. *That raises the possibility that it might not be.* She considered what the conditions of that "if" might be. *If the developer, presumably, is wise enough to engage Baron as consultant.* The note didn't say that Baron, in his role as consultant, would guide the developer in preparing a plan to address the matter, such as by ensuring some alternative means of protecting the endangered plants. The missive merely stated that he would help "ensure a smooth permitting process"—the implication being that Baron would suppress the information about the plant. Conversely, if the developer declined the offer, the implication seemed to be that Emmet would make the presence of these plants widely known in order to drum up opposition.

This alleged offer of services sounded suspiciously like a shakedown.

Kaylee noticed that Emmet was careful to imply that he had proof, but he didn't give enough information that the recipients of the letters could investigate the matter independently. If they took what he said seriously, their only option was to contact Baron. They could also hire another expert to check the area, but that would present the risk of the expert missing whatever flora was in question, and then Baron coming forward with his proof.

So what was the basis for this claim? What was his proof? Did he actually have any?

Kaylee couldn't help but think of the *Orcas Island Triptych*. When Baron had been trying to convince her to carry the note cards, he said something about the original paintings being special to him. And he had apparently said something similar to Clive Randall, explaining why he wouldn't consider selling them back to Justine and Darren or even loan them to the exhibit. But mostly, she thought about the unsettled feeling that those images had given her from the moment she first saw them. Why couldn't she identify the plants?

Could it be that these plants truly were rare and endangered? Or a species that had never been discovered? Or a once-extinct plant that had resurfaced? Was that why she had been unable to classify them or even find them in her standard reference works? Could they truly be that special?

The thought that Baron had been trying to use them for purposes of extorting the developers was abhorrent, of course. But the possibility that he might have been right, that these were plants so unusual that they would not be found anywhere else in the world . . . that was a very special kind of excitement for a plant taxonomist.

Kaylee had to find out for sure, one way or the other.

If Baron was right, his evidence must have come from someplace. She strongly doubted that his expertise in this area would have been anything close to her own, but he must have found the information somewhere. Perhaps Shirley herself had known and told him before she died. Was he already collecting her work at that point? Kaylee would have to nail down the time line.

In the meantime, her own research, while driven by curiosity, had still been rather cursory. She had consulted standard references, but there were certainly more specialized sources that she could also check. And there were colleagues she could call, a list of names already forming in her mind.

Who am I kidding? Kaylee mused. *What I really want to do is get out to the Caslon tract to see exactly what's growing there.*

It was time to call an emergency meeting of the Petal Pushers.

"Road trip!" Jessica sang out as she buckled her seat belt.

"We're only going to the other side of the island," Kaylee said, amused by her friend's enthusiasm.

"I've hardly left my oven in days," Jessica said. "I'll take my excitement where I can find it."

"And what makes you think there are endangered plants there?" Mary asked skeptically, holding an excited Bear on her lap.

Kaylee knew that her explanations up until that point had been vague, but DeeDee, Mary, and Jessica had all agreed to an after-work adventure with few questions asked. "I'm not sure how much I can really go into it. But that's the claim that's been made."

"Oh, this must have something to do with Emmet Baron," Jessica said. "I always love a good murder investigation."

"The police still haven't ruled his death a murder," Kaylee reminded them as she pulled onto Main Street and headed out of Turtle Cove.

DeeDee shrugged. "The police seem to be pretty active for a case that's not murder. They wanted every last detail of every interaction that I'd ever had with the man."

"It's still an unexplained death," Mary said. "They have to take it seriously. And the first days of any investigation are always the most important."

The women continued to discuss the case while they drove, speculating about what might have happened to Emmet Baron that led to his death.

Finally, Mary announced, "The turn is coming up on the left, Kaylee."

Kaylee followed Mary's instructions and turned onto a

single-lane gravel road that was more a path than a street.

"This is it?" Jessica asked as they rolled to a stop by a large lot overgrown with weeds. "I can't imagine we're going to find anything exotic or endangered here."

Kaylee felt the same way. The derelict site was half-covered with crumbling asphalt, and all of the plants in immediate view looked like the usual colonizers of abandoned lots. But ever the scientist, she reminded herself not to let her preconceived notions influence her observation of the subjects at hand.

The four women got out of the car, staring in disbelief at the patch of land. The tract was high up on a hill and a lot smaller than Kaylee had expected. She estimated that about two acres of it, possibly less, was flat enough to build on. Instead of a meadow teeming with native plants, though, the women found the crumbling concrete foundation of an earlier structure.

"The old Harbor View Motel was here before," Mary explained. She held Bear's leash, and he strained to explore this new environment. "Despite the view, it was a dreary little stop on the road." She surveyed the area as if recalling times past. "It went belly-up some thirty years ago, and after it was abandoned it was deemed a health hazard because of the wildlife that moved in. The town eventually took possession and had the buildings condemned and torn down."

Kaylee shielded her eyes as she gazed at the view of the water below. She pulled out her note cards and held them up to compare them to the site.

Jessica came and peeked over Kaylee's shoulder. "This could definitely be the same harbor in the picture." Nodding toward the crumbling concrete, she added, "I can't imagine someone choosing this place to set up their easel and paint, though. Not when there are so many prettier spots."

"Beauty is in the eye of the beholder," DeeDee said. "The whole point of being an artist is seeing things that the rest of us miss."

Jessica shrugged. "Maybe. But what made her come here in the first place?"

"Whatever drew her here, she may have found something significant," Kaylee said. "And we all know that nature will flourish in the most unpromising places."

Kaylee walked toward the edge of the lot, where the land dropped steeply, and held up the card again to compare with the view. She carefully studied the rocks jutting out on the left and the line of rooftops embedded in the hillside that angled down to the water.

"It does match the painting," she said. She squatted down and examined the vegetation, but soon rose again, shaking her head. "But these plants are not where she painted them."

"So what now?" DeeDee asked.

Kaylee grinned. "Treasure hunt."

Pulling out her cell phone, she scrolled to the detailed photos she had taken of the plant in the center panel of the painting. Mary, DeeDee, and Jessica gathered around to peer over her shoulder.

"This is the plant portrait," Kaylee explained. "It was more detailed than the others in the side panels." She zoomed in to focus on a leaf in the painting. "With these broad leaves with the holes, it resembles a monstera plant, except the leaves have narrow tails at their apex. They also have dentate margins, meaning they have teeth along the sides."

"That's our treasure then," DeeDee said.

"Let's each take one edge of the lot and search for something like this," Mary suggested. "Then move back and forth along that line while moving in closer to the center."

"And not just this." Kaylee indicated the image on her phone. "Keep your eye out for anything that seems unusual or just out of place."

"Like litter?" Jessica pointed to a path near the road marred with disposable cups and plastic toys.

Kaylee pulled a face. "I was thinking more botanical in nature. While you three start searching, I'm going to take a video of the area with my phone so I can have something to refer back to."

"I'll keep Bear with me so you don't end up with a shaky video," Mary offered.

With that, they fanned out over the desolate lot.

Starting near the road, Kaylee documented first the ground cover, noting with caution a patch of nettles, but smiling when she saw a string of delicate pink *Linnaea borealis* or twinflower. She next filmed the trees and shrubs. She noted Western red cedar and bitter cherry trees that framed the view of the harbor, along with dense thimbleberry and twinberry plants. Though there was a large portion of the tract that couldn't be reached by foot, Kaylee felt confident that her video gave her a fair representation of the plants growing on the site that she could examine later on the larger screen of her computer.

After finishing her video, Kaylee joined her friends in searching the accessible areas of the tract for Shirley Lucas's mysterious plant. Several fruitless minutes later, they convened in the center of the lot.

"Anybody find anything?" DeeDee asked. "I sure didn't."

"Nothing," Jessica said.

"Me neither," Mary added.

Kaylee was about to give her friends—but mostly herself—a pep talk when she was cut off by the sound of honking. She looked toward the source of the sound and saw that a black truck with tinted windows had pulled up behind her SUV.

An older man emerged and approached the group of women at a fast clip, causing Bear to release a few protective barks. He was clad in work boots, jeans, and a khaki work shirt with the sleeves rolled up to his biceps. Under a cowboy hat, his mirrored aviator sunglasses hid most of his face and reflected the brassy afternoon sun. All Kaylee could see of his face were his thin, down-turned lips and gray stubble on his chin.

"Ladies, what's your business here?" he barked in a rough voice. He stood with his feet apart, hands on his hips.

"Hank Liebling," Mary said. "I recognize you from a few town meetings."

The man removed his sunglasses and set his piercing gaze on Mary. "That's me, but I don't know you. What are you doing on this property?"

"We're the Petal Pushers garden club," Mary responded evenly. "We've come to do a brief survey of what's growing up here."

Liebling peered at each woman in turn with his hard, blue eyes. Then he scanned the tract. "Didn't find anything, I expect. I also expect you're here on account of Emmet Baron. Did he hire you?"

Kaylee shook her head. "Haven't you heard? Emmet Baron is dead."

The older man gave a derisive snort. "Of course I heard. But Baron was a bad penny that kept turning up. I won't believe he's really gone until I see his corpse."

Kaylee tried to cover her shock at his callous response by changing the subject. "You're a developer, aren't you? I gather Emmet Baron had been in contact with you about what he believed was growing out here."

"Is that why you're here?" he demanded. He stalked past them and stared out over the harbor. "You're environmentalists trying to stop the development over a bunch of weeds?"

Kaylee followed him. "We do care about the environment, but that's not our mission here," she said firmly.

Liebling pivoted and gazed down at Kaylee. "You're Bea

Lyons's granddaughter, who took over her flower business. I don't think you're here for a picnic."

"My name is Kaylee Bleu," she said. "We're truly just here to check it out. You're one of the developers who's making a proposal for the site to the town. What do you envision?"

Liebling peered at her with suspicion for a moment, but then said gruffly, "Well, all the submitted proposals are public record. The site is limited, but it's zoned commercial. As you can tell, parking is an issue." He seemed to warm a bit as he described his vision for the development. "I see a small complex of three, maybe four offices. Perfect for a small medical group that wants to expand to the island. Two buildings connected by a breezeway in the center where there'd be picnic tables for patients or employees to sit with a view to the water."

Kaylee nodded. "Sounds like you put a lot of thought into it. And it sounds nice."

"You never did say what you were looking for here," he said, his voice sharpening again.

"I don't know exactly," she said truthfully. "I am consulting with the police, who are aware that Emmet was making certain claims about rare plants found at the site. Emmet was vague, however."

Liebling grunted. "Vague is right. The development business attracts its share of speculators and leeches—people who want to have a piece of your pie. That was Emmet Baron. He came in with this phony scheme that you could smell a mile away. Sure, he might have made some noise that would have triggered extra reviews regarding the environmental impact, but he couldn't have stopped the development. In this sort of situation, it comes down to who has the stamina and resources to see it to the end."

"And would you have the stamina?" Kaylee asked.

He brought his hands to his hips and hooked his thumbs in his belt. "I'm not young and I run a small business, so I don't know if I do. But I definitely would have liked to take him on, just to see what he could come up with."

Kaylee laughed at that, then checked her watch and realized just how much time this little field trip had taken. "I'd better go, but I do have one more question. What proof did Emmet Baron give you to support his claim about the rare plants? Did he talk to you in person, or had he just sent you a letter?"

"Baron never showed his face. I just got the letter a few days ago, so I never saw whatever evidence he apparently had that would trigger a review. I seriously doubt there is any."

Kaylee thanked him for his time, and then she and her friends retreated to her car. Liebling climbed into his truck and drove off.

"Glad you survived that exchange," DeeDee said when they were all back in the SUV. "Old Hank Liebling. He's notorious around the island. I've heard as a boss he's mean as an old mule."

"I can't say I know him all that well," Mary said, "but he did some work on the lighthouse at cost some years ago. It saved the town a good chunk of money on an expensive project. And if it hadn't been done, the lighthouse would have been closed to the public."

Kaylee glanced at DeeDee in the rearview mirror. "Could he have been who we heard arguing with Emmet Baron the other day? The voice was certainly gruff like his."

"I think you might be right," DeeDee answered. "What was he telling you?"

Kaylee started the car and shifted into reverse. "He described his proposal for the site. I got the impression that he didn't take Emmet's threats seriously. However, he did indicate that Emmet's claims would trigger extra attention and review."

"That could certainly hold up the building process," Jessica said. "I wonder what the other developers thought about Emmet's letters."

"I certainly intend to find out," Kaylee said as she returned to the highway and headed back toward Turtle Cove.

The other women chatted as she drove, but Kaylee didn't contribute much. She was unsettled by her conversation with Hank Liebling. His nonchalance about Emmet's claims made her wonder just what the developer might do to make sure Emmet Baron's threats never came to fruition.

10

During the drive back to Turtle Cove, Kaylee also thought of someone else she should ask about the plants in the *Orcas Island Triptych*: Justine Lucas. The artist's granddaughter might be able to confirm the location in the paintings or at least offer some other kind of insight. Kaylee's shoulders slumped as she realized that she had no way of getting in touch with Justine.

As she pulled to a stop in the parking area behind The Flower Patch, where the other women had all left their cars, she turned to DeeDee. "You've known Justine Lucas for a while, right? Do you happen to have her phone number?"

DeeDee shook her head. "Sorry. She might be on our e-mail list, so I could run to the bookstore and try to dig up her e-mail address if you want."

Kaylee shook her head. "It can wait. I'm sure you'd rather get home. I just thought I'd pick her brain about our mystery plant."

"You could always stop by the gallery and ask Clive," DeeDee suggested.

"Good idea," Kaylee said. After thanking her friends for coming with her to the Caslon tract, she said good night to them and drove over to the Randall Gallery. The building was dark, but she'd known it had been a long shot to expect Clive to be there at this hour.

Bear released an excited yip in the back seat and pressed his nose to the window. Kaylee glanced around and realized what had her little dog so excited. The Turtle Cove dog park was only a couple of blocks away. "You really know your way around town, buddy." Kaylee pulled into a parking space.

"Okay, let's go for a walk."

Unable to shake her disappointment at finding nothing in the Caslon tract, Kaylee continued to mull over their visit as she went to the back of the Escape and grabbed a few dog toys and a water dish to put in her tote bag.

She knew from experience that fieldwork was as much a matter of luck as persistence. *Absence of evidence is not evidence of absence,* she reminded herself, recalling the traditional aphorism. One afternoon's trawl through such a large lot could not be considered definitive. *I don't even know if this is the right time of year to find . . . whatever it is that I'm trying to find.*

"No matter, Bear," she said to the dachshund, who had been watching her over the back seat. "We won't give up yet. Ready to go?"

Bear barked a response and scrambled into the SUV's trunk. Kaylee clipped on his leash and set him on the ground. She'd parked near the alley that led to the sandy lot behind the gallery, but when Bear tried to wander down the passage, she tugged on his leash. Emmet Baron's body had been found that way, and it seemed in poor taste to let her dog go sniffing down there. "No, Bear," she commanded. "Come."

However, Bear strained at the leash and managed to get his snout into the weeds growing near the building's foundation. When he finally heeded Kaylee and returned to her side, she was surprised to see that he had something in his mouth. "What have you been hunting, little Bear?" She reached down to take the mystery object from him.

It was a plastic toy—and not just any plastic toy. It was a dragon, one from a set of toy dragons like those DeeDee had shown her, the ones from the Books of the Night series. DeeDee had mentioned they were rare, so what was this dragon doing in the alley beside Clive's gallery?

Her mind swimming with questions, Kaylee put the dragon in

her tote bag and walked Bear along the sidewalk to the dog park.

When Kaylee saw Albert Putnam sitting on a bench reading a book in the dog park, she momentarily considered changing course. She was tired after a long day and stressed from the concerns whirling around in her mind, and she wasn't sure if she was up for trying to make polite conversation with the rather stiff attorney. However, she realized that this was an opportunity to learn more about his relationship with Emmet Baron and anything else he might know that could help her get to the bottom of the possibly fictional plant.

Kaylee let herself and Bear through the gate, and Bear immediately ran over to greet Albert's dog, a white miniature poodle mix wearing a brightly colored bandanna. Kaylee approached the bench where Albert sat. "What are you reading?" she asked.

He must not have noticed Kaylee because he jumped. "Oh, hello," he said when he saw her. He held up *The Night of the Third*. "I kept wondering why the 'third' was the first book in the series," he said with a rueful smile. "It took me a while to understand that 'third' referred to this Ursallan character because of his noble rank. Won't you sit down?"

"I had the same experience." Kaylee took a seat beside Albert. "As the attorney for the press, wouldn't you have read the books already?"

"In truth, I didn't do that much work for Emmet," he said. "There were any number of aspects to his affairs that I . . . took exception to."

Kaylee nodded. "I understand he had some legal issues with the Lucas grandchildren about a book he was doing?"

"I was not representing him in that matter," Albert replied rather stiffly.

"I gather his position was not very strong."

Albert glanced at her. "I don't think it would be appropriate for me to comment since, again, I wasn't part of that suit."

Better change the subject before he shuts me out entirely. "My friend got me into those books," she said, pointing at the one in his hand. "It feels like everyone in town is reading them."

He smiled. "Yes. I had an appointment at the bookstore to see what obligations Emmet might have had regarding the workshop or consignments, and the woman who owns the store talked me into this."

"DeeDee Wilcox. That's my friend." Kaylee glanced up to check on Bear, and she saw that he and Albert's dog were already chasing each other playfully.

"Well, she's good at her job. I actually walked out with a whole stack of new reading material." He patted the hardcover book in his hand. "I have to say, the first chapter starts off with a bang and ends with a real cliff-hanger. I didn't expect that right off the bat."

Kaylee laughed. "DeeDee had to twist my arm to get me to try them. I thought it would be too much fantasy. Now I can hardly put them down." She nodded at Albert's dog, who was running in excited circles with Bear. "What's your dog's name?"

"That's Mitzy. She's three and still has some puppy in her, as you can see."

"And that's Bear," Kaylee said.

Kaylee could see that her dog was enchanted with his new playmate. Albert picked up a stick, waved it until he got the dogs' attention, then tossed it out into the middle of the dog park. Mitzy dashed off and grabbed the stick before Bear had managed to traverse half the distance. He pivoted and joined her on the run back to Albert and Kaylee.

Kaylee reached down to scratch Mitzy, but the pup insisted that Kaylee take the stick and throw it again. Kaylee obliged, sending the dogs on another race.

"So what happens to the press's authors now?" Kaylee asked Albert. "Are they released from their contracts? My understanding was that Griffin Graves had a long, binding agreement in which Puget Press held the option for the first ten books in the series."

Albert sighed. "That depends on the succession plans for the business, if Emmet had any. I'm going over to the mainland tomorrow to go through the papers in his home and office."

Kaylee watched the dogs play. It occurred to her that Griffin had been in town the night that Emmet died. And Emmet held his career hostage. Had Griffin attended the gallery reception? And might he be angry enough, on seeing Emmet, to whack him on the head?

She decided not to voice her questions. Instead, she asked, "Were you able to find anything more at Emmet's house after I left?"

"Some. We found his mortgage documents along with other financial files, which were all fairly well organized. I think if he had kept a will at the house, we would have found it." Albert bent down to take the stick and throw it again for the dogs. "I found correspondence suggesting that he was actively trying to sell a painting that he didn't own. It was another one that he had on loan, this one from a gallery across the island."

"Sell it?" Kaylee asked, shocked. "That must be even worse than using them for collateral."

"I also found angry letters from some editorial freelancers he'd hired. He didn't have a regular staff at Puget Press. His last employee left the press a month or so ago for, quote, 'a real job and paycheck.'"

"I see." Kaylee noted that Albert was chattier now that he was off the clock and decided to push her luck. "Do you know if the coroner or police have classified his death as an accident or homicide yet?"

Albert nodded. "Apparently, he was struck at the base of the skull, a little to the side as if he'd been twisting away when the blow fell. There was some bruising behind his left ear, and the blow appears to have been serious enough to knock him unconscious. Since no blood was found at the scene to indicate that he fell and hit his head—such as on the steps or the grill that was cooling in the back—they're pretty sure someone else was involved."

"I see," Kaylee said, trying to visualize what he was describing. "So the real question is, who hit him? And with what?"

"And what was that person's intent? It appears the injury had an immediate effect on Emmet's state of consciousness, and the attacker did not seek help."

"Could someone have hit him in self-defense?"

Mitzy returned with the stick, and Albert paused to toss it for her again. "That's one possibility. The injury was toward the back of the head, though. If it was in self-defense, it's more likely that Emmet would have been facing whoever hit him, so the injury would have been to the front of his head. But I'm not a criminal lawyer, so I can't really speculate on this."

"I understand. I appreciate your talking to me about it."

Albert nodded, then abruptly switched topics. "Do you have a pet-sitting service to recommend? I'd like to board Mitzy while I go back to the mainland for a couple of days. I'm returning to the cottage I've rented near Eastsound on Sunday, so I thought if I could find a sitter on the island, she wouldn't have to travel on the ferry. She gets a little nervous on the water."

"Why don't you leave her with me?" Kaylee offered. "Bear and I would be delighted to have her company. They appear to be fast friends."

Mitzy was currently doing laps around Bear, who crouched, then pounced on her.

Albert laughed. "That would be really great. I'll drop her off at your shop in the morning."

With another early morning at the shop planned, Kaylee knew that she ought to get to bed at a decent hour. However, after getting supper together for herself and Bear, her mind was still fixated on the mystery plant, and she couldn't wait to start her research. Instead of going to bed, she went to her office and got to work.

With Bear curled up near her feet, she uploaded the detailed pictures she'd taken of the painting that day at Emmet's home, as well as the photos and video she'd captured at the Caslon tract. While she waited for the images to transfer, she did an Internet search for information about the other two developers vying for the Caslon tract, Jim Park and Roger Findley. She jotted down their business addresses and phone numbers, then turned her attention to her images.

She studied them for some time, and then switched to consulting her reference books for leaves that resembled the plant in the painting. She searched for similarities in the leaf holes, the dentate margins, the tips that narrowed to little tails—but nothing was a perfect match.

She compiled a short list of similar plants, hopeful that with more research, perhaps she'd find that one of their obscure varieties was a match. Fortunately, she still shared friendly correspondences with colleagues from the University of Washington who could help her or at least introduce her to other scientists with the knowledge she sought. *It'd be a lot easier if I had a sample of it, though.*

As she reached for a book she'd already looked through twice, Kaylee stopped herself. She felt herself getting more frustrated by the minute, and she knew that she wasn't going to find the answers she was seeking in any of the books she had. With a sigh, she slumped in her chair, staring forlornly at a photo of the triptych.

What am I missing?

11

About an hour before opening the next morning, Kaylee heard a light rapping at The Flower Patch's front door. Hoping it wasn't Deputy Garcia with more bad news, she hurried to answer the knock. She was relieved to see it was Albert, cradling a wriggling Mitzy in the crook of one arm. Bear bounced excitedly at Kaylee's feet, obviously smelling his new friend.

"Good morning," Kaylee said as she opened the door, holding Bear back with one foot to keep him from running out.

"Good morning, Kaylee." Albert stepped in, wheeling an overnight bag and a stuffed canvas tote. Kaylee wondered why he'd found it necessary to bring his luggage in, but who was she to argue?

"Hello," Mary said, approaching from the work area where she'd been putting together more patriotic bouquets. "I'm Mary Bishop."

"Albert Putnam. Pleasure to meet you." Albert reached out to shake Mary's hand. "And this is Mitzy."

"Nice to meet you both." Mary let the little poodle mix sniff her fingers.

"I really appreciate you watching Mitzy," Albert said. "Where would you like her set up?"

"Why don't you come on back?" Kaylee led him from the sales floor into the workroom, Bear excitedly flitting about at their feet the entire way.

Once in the work area, Albert opened the overnight duffel and extracted a collapsible pen, which he deftly set up one-handed. Kaylee suspected that he'd had a lot of practice at it. Then he set

Mitzy inside and gave her a small treat. "She takes to the pen pretty well, so if you feel she is getting too excited you can put her in here. It helps calm her down." He set her dog bed, a couple of microfiber blankets, a few toys, and a bone inside the pen, and then attached a water bottle to the side.

Albert pulled out a set of instructions, encased in a plastic sleeve, and handed it to Kaylee. "That should cover everything you need to know," he said. "She's already eaten this morning, but her other meals are in the tote bag, individually labeled in plastic bags."

"Wow," Kaylee said, smiling, "you certainly are prepared."

"My law school training at work," Albert replied. "You don't know how much this means. I hated the thought of leaving her with strangers."

Bear was sniffing around the outside of the crate, and Albert reached down and gave treats to both dogs. When he stood up, he pulled three note cards from his breast pocket and handed them to Kaylee. "My contact information, in case of emergency. One for the shop, the car, and your home. I have her vet's number on it as well. They are authorized to release her medical information, just in case."

Kaylee pocketed the cards. "Perfect. I don't think you've forgotten anything."

Albert went to the pen and scooped Mitzy up. "Be a good girl, Mitz," he said as he cuddled her, then set her back down. "I'd better get going so I don't miss the ferry."

"I'll walk you out," Kaylee offered. Once she'd locked the door behind him, she returned to the work area and found Mary reading over the instructions with an amused expression on her face.

"Three pages, single-spaced," Mary said. "Kaylee, dear, you could learn a thing or two about spoiling Bear from this man."

"He does set a high bar." Kaylee stared down at Mitzy, who

was sniffing at Bear through the bars of the pen. Bear pawed at the enclosure and whined. "You want in there, Bear? We'll try it, but it's going to be tight."

She lifted the dachshund into the pen and the two dogs immediately began wrestling and playing tug-of-war with Mitzy's various toys.

"Apparently close quarters don't bother them," Mary said with a chuckle.

Kaylee checked her watch. "We've got a little while yet before we open. Do you mind if I step out and see if I can talk with the other two developers vying for the Caslon tract?"

"Not at all. We're caught up on orders." Mary glanced back at the two dogs. "I might just get a cup of coffee and watch these two play for a little while."

"They should charge admission," Kaylee said. "Thanks. I shouldn't be long."

Kaylee headed to her car. Her first stop was Jim Park's office, which was in a converted warehouse on Pacific Street. She tried the front door, but it was locked. Noticing an intercom nearby and realizing she might need to be buzzed in, she walked over and examined the list of businesses with offices in the building. She pressed the button next to *Jim Park & Associates*, but no response came. She pressed the button again, then returned to the door and gave the handle another pull. She nearly stumbled backward when the door opened and a fortysomething man with dark hair and fine features emerged.

"Can I help you?" he asked.

"I'm here to see Jim Park. Can you tell me where his office is?"

"I'm Jim Park, actually."

"Kaylee Bleu. Do you have a few minutes, Mr. Park? There's something I'd like to discuss with you."

"I'm rushing to an appointment. But you're welcome to walk

with me to my car." He pulled a set of car keys from his pocket. "Or if you would like to make an appointment, I have time to sit down with you next week."

Kaylee shook her head. "I just have a quick question. I'm consulting with the police on a matter—"

"Let me guess," he said. "Emmet Baron."

"Yes, actually." Kaylee wondered briefly how surprised she should be that he'd known exactly why she was there. "The sheriff has asked me to check into claims he made regarding—"

"Prehistoric plants thought to be extinct?"

"That's right. I was wondering if you had looked into the matter. Hired an expert, or—"

"What I did," Park said crisply, "is speak with my lawyer, who said I shouldn't answer any questions about rare plants around the Caslon tract. I'm sorry, Ms. Bleu, but I'm taking his advice." He strode toward a luxury electric car parked at the curb. The man walked fast, and Kaylee had to jog to keep up with him.

"Would you at least be willing to tell me what proof Baron offered?" she asked.

Park stopped and faced her. "None. It was an empty threat with no merit. I didn't take him seriously, and I would have countersued if—well, now I've probably said too much, according to my attorney. And here's my car. Have a nice day, Ms. Bleu."

As Park pulled away, Kaylee started after him for a moment, a little shell-shocked by the exchange. The interview had been disappointingly brief, but informative in its way. So Emmet hadn't offered any proof to Liebling or Park. Did that mean there wasn't any?

She headed to her own car and plugged the address for Roger Findley's office into her GPS. She followed the computer's directions, then took a right at a sign that said *Findley Construction*. Kaylee navigated down a narrow driveway, edging past a small bulldozer and various other pieces of heavy machinery. The driveway led to a small, prefabricated ranch house. Beyond the house was an oversize garage with open doors through which Kaylee could see the accoutrements of a woodworking shop.

She rang the doorbell on the house, and the door buzzed to let her in. She was greeted with the smell of cigar smoke and a hoarse voice shouting, "Come to the back!"

Kaylee followed instructions and found Roger Findley at a desk buried under papers and rolled-up blueprints. He stood up when she entered and motioned to a nearby love seat that was also covered in paperwork, which he swept to one side with his hands.

"You're lucky you caught me at my office today," he said. His voice had the deep rumble of a longtime smoker. "What can I do for you, Ms. . . . ?"

"Kaylee Bleu," she said, perching on the edge of the couch cushion. "I'm a plant taxonomist and I'm consulting with the sheriff's office on—"

"Emmet Baron, I'm sure," he said, cutting her off. "The police have already been here. I didn't kill him. I only wish I had an airtight alibi."

"I'm not here to rehash things that the police have covered," she assured him. "I'm just trying to understand what grounds Emmet had for his claim about the Caslon tract."

"If you ask me, I doubt that he had any grounds," Roger said. "But whether there was any truth to his claim didn't matter. Whoever got the job would have to deal with a whole new set of regulations and government oversight because of that claim. That's what's so infuriating." He returned to the chair behind the desk, which creaked heavily when he sat. "When I got his letter, I was ready to pull out, as I told the police. I wasn't going to fight it, and I couldn't afford to pay him for his 'consulting services.'" He put air quotes around the words.

"Did you recognize the rare plants Emmet Baron claimed grew on the Caslon tract site?"

"Have you seen the site?" When Kaylee nodded, he continued. "Then you know it was all bluster. But Baron was going to ruin me before I even got a foothold. And I don't believe for a minute that he was going to stop at the Caslon tract. That man was a mosquito, always ready to bite."

"So I've heard." Kaylee stood up. "Thank you, Mr. Findley. If you don't mind my asking, what were you planning to propose for the land?"

He pointed to an architectural drawing pinned to the wall. "A commercial kitchen that could be rented by the hour or day," he said gruffly. "Plenty of people want to become professional caterers or bakers or whatnot these days. You can't just make stuff in your home kitchen if it doesn't meet state regulations. My proposal was for a commercial kitchen that vendors could rent." His voice warmed slightly with enthusiasm. "Say you make frozen pizzas to sell, you might need to only rent it for one day a week, or one day a month. This kitchen would have a couple of workstations, commercial ovens, dishwashers, freezers, and refrigerators. I've already got a list of folks who'd pay to use it."

"That sounds like a solid proposal," Kaylee said.

He sighed, and his tone turned bitter once again. "Yeah, it was. It would support local businesses and generate tax revenue for the area without bringing in a lot of traffic to flood the roads."

"It sounds like you put a lot of thought into it."

"It still could work if I don't have this threat hanging over me. I mean, it's a shame Baron is dead, but it does change things. At least, one would hope it does." He narrowed his eyes as if preparing to weigh her reaction.

Kaylee wasn't sure what response he wanted. "As I said, Mr. Findley, I'm just checking into this because the police asked me to."

"Uh-huh," he said, his voice heavy with skepticism. "I hope that's true, Ms. Bleu—that you're just helping out and not trying to pick up where Emmet Baron left off."

Kaylee declined to dignify that with a response, but she felt his glare following her as she left.

12

$\mathbf{K}$aylee returned to the shop just as the flow of customers started increasing. She and Mary remained busy for several hours, but after giving Mary a much-deserved long lunch, Kaylee snuck out during an afternoon lull to visit Between the Lines. She wanted to ask DeeDee about the dragon figure she'd found—or rather, the one Bear had found. Besides, the workshop was scheduled to have its first session, and Kaylee wondered if she might get a chance to meet Griffin Graves.

When she entered the store, she saw a group of people gathered in the workshop area, but no other customers. DeeDee, however, was wearing a worried expression when she came to greet Kaylee at the door.

"Thank goodness you're here," DeeDee whispered. "Help me corral these people. They keep wandering all over like they own the place."

"Is everything okay?" Kaylee asked.

DeeDee quickly glanced over her shoulder to make sure no one else was in earshot, then leaned closer to Kaylee. "Griffin's late. He's been in town all week, and he's been to the shop a few times, so it's not like he got lost. It's probably nothing, but still, given everything that's happened . . ."

"I'm sure everything's fine," Kaylee said. "He most likely just got held up."

"You're probably right. Come on. I've set out refreshments." DeeDee led the way back to the workshop area where the six participants were gathered around a conference table. The sound of nervous chatter reminded Kaylee of the excitement she used to feel on the first day of classes, as students, refreshed after a term break, were expectant and eager.

Kaylee's tall plants segmented off the back quarter of the shop, with a small passageway through the middle. On one side of the space was the conference table, and on the other side was an assortment of chairs set off in groups.

"That was Griffin's suggestion at dinner last night," DeeDee said, indicating the seating areas. "He wants to have some small brainstorming sessions. I think it feels more private this way too."

"This is great. You've set things up perfectly."

"Could you keep an eye on things in here for a minute and make sure nobody wanders off? I need to make a phone call."

"Of course," Kaylee said. While DeeDee bustled off, Kaylee leaned over to adjust the moss at the base of one of the plants. As she did, a young woman with bright eyes, a pixie haircut, and a string of small silver hoops along the side of one ear came over and introduced herself.

"Welcome. I'm Jules," she said, offering her hand to shake. "Please help yourself to coffee."

Kaylee smiled. *If Griffin doesn't show up, I'm sure this young woman will take charge.* "Nice to meet you. I'm Kaylee, but I'm not a writer. I'm just here to tend to the plants."

"The *Monstera deliciosa*?" Jules's face brightened. "I work in an interior design shop where we have these exact same plants around. It puts people at ease and they spend more money." She shrugged. "Or that's what the boss tells me."

Kaylee chuckled. "And here I thought people were buying Griffin's books because DeeDee was doing such a good job selling them."

Jules grinned. "I'm sure that helps. Anyway, the monstera are perfect for the weekend's topic. They are exactly what I imagined would grow on Ellaryn and Netiril. Especially Ellaryn. Oh, those are the twin planets in Griffin's books."

"I know. I'm reading them myself, actually. I prefer Ellaryn, where the dragons and all those gorgeous plants live."

"That makes sense, given your profession."

Kaylee poured herself a cup of coffee from the carafe DeeDee had set out and grabbed a pastry that had probably come from Death by Chocolate. "Do you write mysteries or fantasy?"

"Regency romance, actually. But I love the Books of the Night—and world building is just as important in historical fiction as it is in fantasy or science fiction. You still have to know how much background to include without slowing down the story. The difference is that I work within a real setting and have to get the details right or the history buffs will be on my case."

Kaylee was about to respond, but DeeDee bustled into the meeting area carrying notebooks and pens, which she set out at the table for the participants. After she was done, she began handing out name tags. "Jamie?"

A tall, stooped man shyly stepped forward and accepted his tag. He put it on upside down, which no one commented on. Kaylee wondered if it was something that would come up in one of the later books she had yet to read.

"Kent? Zach?" Two twentysomething men who had been in rapt conversation in a corner accepted their name tags from DeeDee. "Rita?"

The only writer who seemed to be over thirty stood up with a quiet groan and edged around from behind Kent and Zach to accept hers. Rita had a shock of gray curly hair held back with a paisley scarf, and assorted silver bangles on her arm clinked against each other as she moved.

"Jules?"

Kaylee's new friend went to take her tag.

"And Phyllis?"

"Actually, it's Magdalene," a tall, muscular woman said drily. "Can I have mine redone please?" She was dressed in a black T-shirt and black jeans. Her long, sandy-brown hair hung in a braid down her back. Kaylee recognized Magdalene as the name of a character in the Night series and wondered if there was some connection there.

"One moment," DeeDee said, unfazed, and she retreated once again to her office.

Rita edged over to Magdalene and engaged her in a discussion about taking on character personas. Apparently the woman's renaming of herself was indeed some sort of homage to the series. Jules's attention was drawn to Rita and Magdalene too, so Kaylee took the moment to slip away and join DeeDee in her office.

"It seems like you've got an interesting group," Kaylee said brightly.

"Writers are always an interesting group," DeeDee said as she waited for her printer to warm up.

"Before you have to go host them again, guess what I found."

"A living, growing, once-extinct plant?" DeeDee asked facetiously.

"No. Not yet, anyway. A dragon toy, like the ones you showed me. Are you missing one? Or did you sell one?"

DeeDee spared her a curious glance as her printer hummed to life. "No, I still have them all. I couldn't say where yours came from. Maybe Emmet lost it?"

Kaylee realized with a start that this was a solid theory. After all, Bear had found the toy not far from where Emmet Baron had died.

"You know, I am sorry he's dead," DeeDee said thoughtfully. "I'm sorry he died the way he did. That was awful. But all the same, if he were alive, he'd be here now souring the atmosphere." She peered around the open door of her office. "Look at them.

They're all eager, and they're all bonding with one another."

"I can see how having someone with the wrong energy could sour the creative vibe," Kaylee said. "Speaking of creative vibes, have you heard from Griffin?"

DeeDee shook her head, then grabbed Magdalene's new name tag off the printer and headed back to the workshop area with Kaylee on her heels.

When Magdalene accepted her name tag, she, too, put it on upside down.

"It's from the third book," DeeDee explained to Kaylee. "*The Night of the Eighth.*"

Kaylee's phone buzzed, and she pulled it out to read the text from Mary. *Will you be long? Afternoon rush is in full force.*

A wave of guilt flooded Kaylee, and she realized that she owed Mary more than a long lunch for the hard work she'd been putting in lately. "I've got to run," she said to DeeDee.

"Okay." DeeDee glanced beyond her toward the window, and relief swept over her face. "Griffin is coming," she announced to the room.

All the workshop participants turned toward the window, nearly in unison.

Kaylee sighed. Eager as she was to meet the author, Mary needed her. She slipped out the back and returned to The Flower Patch.

Exhausted from their rambunctious playing at the shop all day Friday, Bear and Mitzy were fairly subdued that evening when Kaylee brought them back to Wildflower Cottage. After investigating her new surroundings for a few minutes and eating a good dinner, Mitzy settled herself onto the dog bed Kaylee had brought along from the shop and Bear curled up on his own cushion nearby.

The new best friends must have slept well, because they were ready to start their day at the crack of dawn. Kaylee decided that it was a good time to check on the flower boxes she and Mary had created for Main Street, so she leashed the dogs, loaded them and their supplies in her SUV, and drove into Turtle Cove.

After a quick stop at The Flower Patch for some trimmers and a watering can, Kaylee brought the dogs with her as she deadheaded the plants and gave each window box a good watering. Although she knew it was a gamble to bring the two high-energy pups along on her errand, she also knew they'd enjoy sniffing each building foundation, lamppost, and bicycle rack along the way—and they did exactly that. It was a small sacrifice to work one-handed while her other hand held their leashes.

Once the street boxes were spruced up, they returned to the shop. Mary wasn't due in until half an hour before opening time, so Kaylee put together the handful of special orders scheduled for pickup that day while Bear and Mitzy played happily together in the pen in the work area. When the bouquets were completed, Kaylee saw that she had more than an hour until opening—just enough time to stop by the Randall Gallery to see if Clive could give her any further information about the *Orcas Island Triptych*.

After checking the dogs' water and texting Mary to let her know where she was going in case it took longer than expected, she left the flower shop and locked the door behind her. The sun was shining and the sea air was crisp, so Kaylee enjoyed every step of her walk to the gallery. When she arrived, she could see interior lights on, so even though the *Closed* sign was up, she felt emboldened to rap on the glass door.

Through the front door's large window, Kaylee watched as Clive stepped out of his office with a questioning expression on his face. He relaxed when he saw Kaylee.

"I'm sorry to drop in so early," she said as she entered the shop.

"It's no trouble at all," Clive said. "What brings you by?"

Instead of answering right away, Kaylee found herself again enchanted by the beauty of Shirley Lucas's art. "It's funny," she said. "They look different today. It must be the light. They take on a whole new character."

Clive came to stand beside her near *Truth or Lavendare.* "You are perceptive, Kaylee. One thing Shirley understood was the effect of light on color, and she knew how to use that when she mixed her oils."

Kaylee nodded. "Which brings me to the question I came to ask: Why were the note cards of the *Orcas Island Triptych* such poor reproductions? If Emmet was trying to sell them —"

"Kaylee, I think you are being a little too literal about what Emmet was peddling," Clive interrupted. "First off, the images were bad because Emmet took the photos himself. I'm sure he used a cheap camera and didn't even bother trying to get the paintings into natural light. Second, Emmet was never actually selling what he claimed to be. I'm sure he had an ulterior motive."

Kaylee wondered whether Clive knew about Emmet's threat to the developers of the Caslon tract. "And what might that be?"

"If I had to guess, I would say that Emmet was trying to drum up interest in the triptych so he could sell it at a profit."

"Then why not loan it to you for the retrospective?"

Clive shrugged. "He was also ornery and spiteful. A check he wrote to me was no good, and I had to keep after him about it. He still owed me quite a bit of money when he died. Perhaps he thought that if I had the triptych here, I'd hold it hostage. Well, he got the last laugh, didn't he? The gallery was closed by the police just when traffic should have spiked. We've reopened, but I feel like we've lost momentum." Clive sighed. "I wanted this for the kids—and speak of the devil!"

Kaylee followed his gaze to see Justine waving at them. Clive opened the door for the newcomer.

"Kaylee, so nice to see you!" Justine gushed. "I hope I'm not interrupting anything."

"You're never an interruption, Justine," Clive assured her.

"Good." Justine took a breath. "I have a request. Given the circumstances, it may seem inappropriate."

"Anything for you," Clive said.

"As you know, we were trying to buy back the triptych from Baron. He kept claiming he had other buyers willing to offer better prices, though. I was wondering—and I understand if this is confidential information—but do you know who these other buyers were? Would it be possible for us to speak with them directly?"

Clive rubbed his jaw. "We were just pondering what Emmet's plans for the triptych might have been. I thought that might be why he had those note cards made up. Not to sell them, but to sell the triptych."

Mention of the note cards caused Justine's face to crease in disapproval. She began walking slowly around the perimeter of the gallery. *Probably to cool her temper,* Kaylee thought.

When Justine joined them again, she asked, "But what about these other buyers?"

Clive shook his head. "I'm sorry, but he wasn't going through me. I've heard nothing about other buyers."

Justine raised her eyebrows. "Is there any way that you might be able to find out?"

"I can try. It's true that the art world can be a small one." He hesitated. "But I should point out that this might be a delicate time for such inquiries. While Darren is . . ."

"Still under suspicion of murder?" Justine huffed. "The

police didn't officially charge him. They just told him not to leave the island. I know he's innocent. I don't care what it looks like." Her face flushed.

"Maybe I can help," Kaylee said. Justine and Clive raised skeptical eyebrows. "I have an in with the lawyer appointed to oversee his estate, Albert Putnam. I'm watching his dog while he's on the mainland going through Emmet's other house and office."

Justine's uncertain expression softened into a sad smile. "I'll take anything that would help. Thanks." She gestured around the gallery. "Shirley was so remarkable. And she was just as creative in her gardening."

"That elaborate garden," Clive said appreciatively. "Is your grandfather keeping it up?"

"He tries." Justine turned to Kaylee. "My grandparents divorced years ago, but they remained friends and Shirley kept Lucas as her last name. When my grandmother was dying, my grandfather moved back into the house to take care of her. He lives there now."

"I bet the garden is fantastic," Kaylee said. "I wonder if the more unusual plants she painted came from her garden."

"Would you like to see it?" Justine clapped her hands excitedly. "Why don't you come with me tomorrow? Grandpa lives in Dungeness. I'm taking the noon high-speed ferry over so I can bring him back here. He has a very calming effect on Darren. Being angry all the time isn't really helping my brother's case."

"Can I bring my dog? I don't like to leave him too long." Mitzy would be reuniting with Albert the next morning. Bear might like a little adventure to take the sting off of being separated from his new friend.

"Of course," Justine answered immediately. "Grandpa loves animals. I'll meet you at the ferry. Give me your number and I'll text you if anything changes."

As Kaylee rattled off her cell phone number, a sense of giddiness swept over her, and she realized just how eager she was to see Shirley Lucas's garden. Would it hold any clues that could help her uncover the mysteries of the *Orcas Island Triptych*?

13

Just a few minutes before opening time, Kaylee let herself in the back door of The Flower Patch. In the work area, Mary was loading her arms with beautiful lavender-and-cedar wreaths.

"I think you might still have room for the kitchen sink," Kaylee said with a chuckle, rushing forward to help her friend. "Give me some of those."

"Just trying to save myself a trip." Mary off-loaded a few of the wreaths into Kaylee's hands. "I thought we could use something other than red, white, and blue out on the sales floor."

"Great idea," Kaylee said as they made their way to the front of the shop. "There'll be a lot of tourists in town, and hopefully they'll want to bring home a less seasonal souvenir." She glanced down and noticed that Mary had tied wine-colored raffia bows onto each wreath. "The raffia is a perfect touch."

"Thanks, boss."

The women rearranged a few items on a display to accommodate the new additions, and then Kaylee went to unlock the front door. As she did, she realized it was rather quiet in the shop. "Where are Bear and Mitzy?" she asked.

"In the sitting room," Mary answered. "They got tired of being cooped up, so I tried letting them out. Mitzy, it turns out, is a natural watchdog. She'd come barking whenever someone walked past the window. I gave them each a bone, so they should be happy for a while."

"I hope they haven't been too much of a bother."

Mary shook her head, smiling. "I think they're settled now."

The front door chimed with the first customers of the day, and Kaylee peered over the wreath display. Rita, Jules, and Magdalene from the writing workshop stepped in and fanned out to view the potted houseplants for sale throughout The Flower Patch.

Jules and Rita kept up some argumentative banter as they flitted from plant to plant, while Magdalene, taller than the others by half a head, hung back. She seemed particularly pasty and wan, and Kaylee wondered if she was feeling ill.

"There's so much to choose from," Kaylee overheard Rita say. Her comment was accompanied by the melodic clinking of her excessive bangles. "We've got to hurry, though. We only have fifteen minutes until our break is over."

Kaylee stepped forward. "May I help you ladies?"

"We're trying to find a gift for Griffin," Jules explained. "Something a little different, but not too fussy."

"Hmm." Kaylee thought for a moment, then showed them a display of terra-cotta planters with a variety of succulents, but that suggestion was met with silence.

"We already ruled them out," Rita said. "Too common."

Kaylee ran her gaze around the main floor. "I have a couple of varieties of dieffenbachia." She waved them over to a corner. "I particularly like this one, *Dieffenbachia seguine.*"

"Another common one," Jules said. "Though on the upside, it's poisonous!" She smiled wickedly. "That's the kind of thing that writers ought to always be on the lookout for, don't you think?"

Kaylee pointed to the plant in question. "This one has variegated leaves, as you can see. But yes, it is poisonous. Do you know if Griffin has pets? If he does, and they have a tendency to chew on plants, this might not be a good choice." She stepped back, thinking.

"Aren't you the mystery writer here?" Jules nudged Rita with her elbow. "Take note."

Rita chuckled. "Poison's overrated," she said drily.

Kaylee scrutinized the surrounding plants. "Or there's this one we've just started carrying, the *Calathea ornata*. The pinstripe plant. It has these pink and green stripes on top and a reddish tint underneath." She flipped over the leaf to show the color variation.

Jules's eyes lit up, and she turned to her friends. "It's perfect! I could totally see it growing on Ellaryn. Can you repot it for us? We'd like to present it to him at the reading on the last day."

"Didn't you say you wanted your set of dragons to decorate the plant, Magdalene?" Rita asked.

Magdalene opened her oversize shoulder bag and started rooting around. She pulled out a red-and-yellow serpentine dragon with diamond-pattern scales and a sand-colored one that was broad and sported a ridged back. She handed them to Rita and continued searching her bag, then brought out an emerald-green dragon that had one paw up, catlike. She handed that one to Jules, then went back to digging in her purse.

Jules opened her own bag and pulled out a blue dragon, identical to the one Kaylee and Bear had found by the gallery.

"The Ellarynian dragons," Kaylee said. "I understand there was just a limited run of these."

"That's right," Magdalene said, her voice edged slightly with hostility. "It was another way Emmet Baron was capitalizing on Griffin's creativity."

"And despite that," Jules said with a chuckle, "there are a few still in stores on the island, and we've been on a treasure hunt to find them all."

Kaylee gathered up the four figurines. "If you want to pick out a pot that you like, I think I can rig up a way to secure the dragons inside."

Jules was given the task of picking out the pot, while Magdalene left to go bring her car around to make loading the plant easier. Rita stood near Kaylee as they watched Magdalene stomp out the door.

"Poor kid." Rita shook her head. "She's in love. She's the best writer of the bunch, but I think she frightens Griffin a bit. He's managed to redirect her from writing fan fiction—you know, stories based on his characters and worlds—to developing her own stuff. Let me tell you, her original stories are wild and, frankly, terrific . . . if a little disorganized. He wants her to work on sequential plotting. As for me, he says I need to focus on 'coherent world building.' Meaning," she said with a grin, "my creative chops need honing."

Kaylee was surprised by Rita's candor. "I'm sure all writers have areas they need to work on," she said diplomatically.

Rita laughed again. "Oh, I have no illusions. I love writing, but I know I will never be a published author. I came because I love the books, and I wanted to do something different with my vacation this year."

Jules returned, her selected planter in tow. Instead of a clay pot, she had chosen a slatted cedar box, into which the plant's original plastic pot fit perfectly. "I think this will be just right," she said with satisfaction. "Nice and natural and a little manly."

Kaylee took it to the work area behind the front counter. She nestled moss around the base of the plant to hide the dirt and fill in the gaps between planter and box. Next, she used plastic ties and stem supports to arrange the dragon figurines among the leaves.

"That's wonderful," Rita said with a smile. She paid for the plant. Kaylee was handing Rita her change when Magdalene honked her horn out front.

Jules swept the cedar box into her arms and called "Thanks again!" as she hurried to meet Magdalene. Rita gave a wave as she followed Jules out the door.

Kaylee watched them through the front windows for a moment as they loaded the plant into the back of Magdalene's ancient hatchback. Seeing the cedar box nestled amid the litter of books, papers, and blankets, she was reminded briefly of her college days, when her own trunk had always been stuffed with textbooks, work gloves, and bags for collecting plant samples.

Her nostalgia turned to annoyance when she realized that, despite all that training, she still couldn't identify the mystery plant in Shirley Lucas's painting.

Business that day ebbed and flowed, but things slowed down enough by midafternoon that Kaylee sent Mary home to spend some quality time with Herb. Only a few more people came in before closing time, so Kaylee was able to get the shop cleaned up and ready to reopen Monday. The dogs, who had spent the day either playing in the sitting room or playing in the pen in the work area, were napping soundly.

The dogs were sleeping so peacefully that she decided to leave them while she ran next door to Death by Chocolate to see Jessica. When she arrived, she found a young man with a backpack staring dejectedly at the bakery's *Closed* sign. Kaylee immediately recognized Griffin Graves from his photograph on the back covers of his books. As in the picture, his messy brown hair was swept across his forehead, the telltale sign of someone who absently ran his fingers through his hair as he contemplated the universe.

"You look like you could use some chocolate," Kaylee said, knocking on the door.

"It's closed," Griffin grumbled.

"I bet we can twist the owner's arm." Kaylee clasped her hands in a begging motion when Jessica opened the door. "Please, ma'am, can we have some sweets?"

"I might have a few scraps for you. Come on in." Jessica smiled and beckoned them inside.

Kaylee stepped into the darkened café, followed by Griffin, who glanced around apprehensively. Kaylee introduced herself and Jessica, explaining that they were both good friends of his hostess, DeeDee. "I'm quite sure she would want us to take care of you."

"Please come sit," Jessica added. As Kaylee and Griffin sat down at a table, she asked, "Coffee? I'll bring out some chocolate pound cake and *pain au chocolat*."

Kaylee could see Griffin's eyes light up just a bit, but he said, "I really don't want to put you to any trouble."

"No trouble at all." Jessica cast an appraising gaze over the author. "You're hoarse. Do you have a sore throat? I can bring you tea instead of coffee."

Griffin coughed. "Tea would be lovely, thank you. I've been talking all day. We started yesterday afternoon, but today was the first full day."

"We're eager to hear how it's going," Kaylee said. "It's a big deal for DeeDee, and we're fans of your series too."

Soon Jessica had brought them a scrumptious array of treats and drinks. Kaylee watched Griffin eagerly start to reach for a croissant and then catch himself and gesture for the ladies to start. There was something endearingly boyish about the motion. Kaylee picked up the platter and presented it to him, inviting him to help himself.

"So what do you think of your students?" Kaylee asked after everyone had enjoyed a bite or two. "Do you have a good group?"

Griffin hesitated briefly before nodding. "Yes, they're very

. . . enthusiastic. But I'm afraid I don't have much experience as a teacher. And I'm not really used to telling people what to do."

"Have you done any teaching before this?" Jessica asked.

Even in the dimness of the shop, the blush creeping over Griffin's face was clear. "Actually, I haven't. And I explained that to my publisher and then to DeeDee, but Emmet said I had a responsibility to promote the books, and DeeDee said it would be fine—I'd just need to talk about my own process. She says that every writer needs to find what works for them, but that it can be helpful just to hear about someone else's experience."

"I'm sure she's right," Kaylee said encouragingly. "Every writer needs to find their own voice. The fact is that you have clearly found what works for you. And that's why those people have signed up for your workshop. You've succeeded in writing something that speaks to them, and they're eager for a glimpse into how you did it."

Seemingly reassured, Griffin reached for another helping of dessert. "That may be. In any case, I've been cramming how-to-write and how-to-teach-writing books for the past three weeks trying to get ready for this."

"And did they help?" Jessica asked.

"I'm not sure. I hope so. Most of what we did today was based on ideas I got from them."

"Like what?" Kaylee sipped at her decaf coffee.

"Many of the books talked about freewriting as a good exercise to generate ideas and to start getting words onto the page, so we spent quite a lot of time on that," Griffin explained. "First I had them do it individually, then I divided them into two groups of three to share and discuss. And then we all did some brainstorming as a group."

"And were you happy with the results?" Jessica asked.

"Actually, I was." His face lit up. "One of the groups had

actually started developing this collaborative world that involved human beings living alongside intelligent dinosaurs."

Jessica's eyebrows went up. "Dinosaurs?"

"Fantasy is the prevalent genre for these writers," Griffin explained. "But the point is that, even though this wasn't really what I expected them to do right then, world building is a big focus of the workshop and the fact that they went in that direction spontaneously struck me as a really good sign. And then when we all came together, the whole group got excited by the idea. They've decided to call themselves the Dino-Writes." There was a shy pride in his voice as he said this.

"That's great," Kaylee said. "It sounds like they've really come together as a group."

"It's also thrown off all my planning," Griffin added with a rueful chuckle. "The fact that they came up with this on their own feels like a real opportunity, and I want to continue to build on it for the rest of the workshop. But now I have to adjust all my lesson plans to accommodate that."

"Spoken like a born teacher," Jessica said. "I'm sure your students are having a wonderful time."

"They certainly seem to be." He pointed to his backpack. "And they're producing lots of pages too."

"So this workshop is a lot of work for you," Jessica said. "I hope you've been able to set aside time for your own endeavors. Moira's place seems like a wonderful retreat for a creative spirit."

Tapping his lips with a napkin, Griffin shook his head. "I haven't had a spare moment, even though I've been here all week. But sometimes we have to pay a price for our art." An ironic gleam flashed in his eyes.

Kaylee chuckled. "I think Jess and I both understand that."

"I will admit that it hasn't been all work this week," Griffin said. "I did find time to view the Shirley Lucas retrospective.

Have you seen it?"

"Yes!" Jessica exclaimed. "It's fantastic, isn't it?"

Griffin nodded, his mouth curving into a bright smile. "Her paintings were an early inspiration for my series. I've admired her work ever since I first saw one of her paintings when I was in college." His eyes sparkled. "And now I'm going to buy one. It's a splurge, but something in her work inspires me. I just had to have the piece, and I can finally afford it."

"That's wonderful. Which painting do you have your eye on?" Jessica asked.

"I put a deposit down on one called *Truth or Lavendare*. I don't suppose you remember it."

"Remember it? I practically live it." She gestured toward the lavender geranium on the café's front counter. "Meet Oliver."

Griffin laughed. "There's a very close resemblance, isn't there?"

"My husband will be so glad to hear I won't be spending our retirement fund on a painting," Jessica said with a chuckle.

They fell into an easy silence for a few moments as they continued eating and drinking. Kaylee spoke next. "Griffin, I wanted to express my condolences on the death of your publisher. I hope that hasn't thrown a pall over the weekend for you."

"Thank you," he replied carefully. "I can't say that Emmet and I were close, but it is strange to be without him now."

Kaylee and Jessica exchanged a glance. Kaylee decided to push her luck. "It sounds like he wasn't really a mentor to you. But he gave you your start?"

Griffin sighed and looked down into his lap. When he raised his head again, he said, "I was very naive. I didn't know anything about getting published or getting an agent or anything like that. I just drew up a list of publishers—mostly local, thinking I'd have a better chance with them—and sent my stuff out blind. I didn't even research what kinds of things each house published. Puget

Press was the first to respond, and I was so excited about getting published that I would have agreed to anything." He took a deep breath. "In fact, I did agree to anything. I've had plenty of agents and other publishers scold me for the contractual terms I agreed to. But I signed. And I accepted the money."

Kaylee had the sense that Griffin had grown accustomed to telling this story. "And you couldn't just switch to another publisher once you knew better, could you?"

Griffin shook his head. "I have signed on with an agent now, one of the best, and she's been trying to get me out of the contract. But she says it's ironclad. I think she kind of admires it in a way, not that she isn't doing her best to break it. The problem is that if I don't fulfill the terms, I might lose the rights to the Books of the Night series. I couldn't write them for someone else, nor could anyone else publish them. And I've invested too much into that series to see that happen. Emmet could have even brought in other writers to do the books. He'd been threatening to do that anyway, trying to bully me." The young man's fists balled up in frustration.

"Well, he can't do that now," Jessica said gently. "Maybe there's a silver lining here, if you'll be able to get out of your contract now."

"I hope so," Griffin said earnestly.

Although the young author's delivery of the statement was guileless, the words made Kaylee wonder how far someone might go to free themselves from the clutches of one of Emmet Baron's ironclad contracts.

14

When Kaylee returned to The Flower Patch a short time later to collect the dogs, she nearly collided with Reese on the sidewalk out front. Startled, she put out a hand to steady herself, and it landed on the handsome handyman's arm, which was strong and tanned from hours working in the summer sun. She felt a warm glow that, she had to admit, wasn't courtesy of the sun.

"Nice to know you're in such a hurry to meet me," he said, a smile lighting up his face.

"What?" Kaylee asked, confusion replacing the pleasant sensation she'd just felt.

Reese raised an eyebrow. "I'm here to fix that upstairs door. You told me it was sticking again."

Embarrassment washed over Kaylee as she realized she'd completely forgotten asking Reese to stop by that evening. She flashed a quick grin. "Thanks for coming." She walked up the porch steps and unlocked the door, then she pushed it open. She nearly closed it again when she caught sight of two small dogs madly tearing around the shop in play. "Bear! Mitzy!" she hollered, but they paid her no mind.

"Mitzy?" Reese asked with interest.

"Long story." Kaylee shooed Reese inside and shut the door so the pups couldn't run out into the street. She made her way to the counter where she kept a stash of dog cookies, then asked loudly, "Who wants a treat?"

That brought both dogs to a halt in front of her, though they still quivered with suppressed energy. After downing their treats in quick gulps, they were off again.

With a cursory glance around the shop, Kaylee determined that, at least so far, their romping hadn't led to any serious damage. Reese, meanwhile, was trying to get Bear's attention. Squatting down and slapping his thighs, he said, "Here, buddy. Who's your friend, Bear? Who's this?" But even though Reese was one of Bear's favorite humans, even he couldn't compete with Mitzy's allure.

Kaylee couldn't help laughing. "I'm sorry, but I think we're going to have to postpone this. I'd better get these two over to the dog park before they break something. I'm sorry to have wasted your time coming here."

Reese stood. "Do you mind if I tag along? I'd prefer the dog park to fixing a sticky door any day."

Once leashed and out the door, Bear and Mitzy calmed down a bit, or at least became more focused. They quickly realized where they were headed, however, and that realization infused new life into them. They both strained at the leash to get to the park sooner, though occasionally stopping short to sniff the closest plants peeking through the seams in the sidewalk.

"So who's Bear's new friend?" Reese asked as they walked.

"Mitzy belongs to Albert Putnam, the attorney. Do you know him?"

"Albert Putnam?" Reese shook his head. "No, I don't think I do."

Kaylee launched into an explanation about how she'd come to be Mitzy's dog sitter, which led to her sharing everything she knew — and didn't know — about Emmet Baron, the *Orcas Island Triptych*, and the letters to the developers. She found herself telling Reese about the possibility of discovering some plants thought to be extinct. She'd barely begun when they arrived at the dog park.

"That's interesting," Reese said, holding the gate open for Kaylee and the dogs. "I've heard of extinct animals being found to still be alive, but never plants."

"It does happen," Kaylee assured him. "They found one in Vermont not too long ago. But there are more people looking for animals than there are for plants, and in my experience the media is much more likely to play up a story about animals. But you're right—it's not exactly common, which is why it would be so exciting if it were true."

Bear and Mitzy yipped joyously as they were let off their leashes. While they sprinted off to chase each other and smell the far reaches of the fenced park, Kaylee and Reese sat on the bench.

"If it were true, would it really block the development of the Caslon tract?" Reese asked.

Kaylee sighed. "It's hard to say. The legal status of endangered flora is nowhere near as clear as it is for endangered animals. I think a strong case could be made for at least having some kind of study implemented before anything irrevocable is done to the property. I'd hope so, at least."

"Wouldn't it be easier to protect an endangered plant?" Reese asked. "I mean, animals move around and you have to consider their whole habitat. But with plants, couldn't you just transplant them somewhere else? Either into a greenhouse or somewhere in the wild with similar soil? I'm just wondering what the appropriate provisions might be."

"The question of what constitutes 'appropriate provision' is something that would certainly have to be addressed. And without knowing more about the plants themselves—what they are, what they need—it's impossible to settle that question." She sighed. "And they may not be there at all. But I do wonder if the developers in question would share your enlightened attitude."

"Some more than others, maybe. I've worked with all of them to some degree. I'm happy to tell you what I can about them."

"That would be really helpful," Kaylee said, gratitude coursing through her. "I didn't have the best interaction with any of them."

"Let's start with Hank. What did you make of him?"

"He seemed rather abrasive to tell you the truth."

Reese nodded. "That's how most people find him. In fairness, I have to say that he's somewhat less so when you get to know him better. Part of it's his age. He's been around a long time and has reached the point where he figures that he just doesn't have to give a hoot if he doesn't want to. I bet if he doesn't get the contract for the Caslon tract, he'll probably just retire."

"So he's not emotionally invested," Kaylee said thoughtfully.

Reese shook his head. "Don't confuse not caring what people think with not caring about the community. What most people don't realize is that he's actually very civic-minded. In fact, he's done a lot of good for Orcas Island over the years, though he doesn't get much credit. Granted, his ideas these days about what's good for the community are rather old-fashioned, and they are always bound up with what's also good for Hank Liebling, but don't make the mistake of thinking that he's entirely self-serving. I know of several cases where he has accepted a smaller return on his investment in order to create something that was better for the community overall." He stood. "Want to stroll a little?"

"Sure." Kaylee joined him and they began circling the enclosure. "Now, what about Jim Park?"

Reese was quiet for a moment, seemingly gathering his thoughts. "In some ways, Jim is like Hank was twenty years ago. He's definitely the most ambitious of the three. Hank's getting on and can think about retirement, but Jim's still hungry. He has some of Hank's civic-mindedness, but in my opinion—and I want to stress that this is just me—I get the sense that he's somewhat more strategic about it. I wouldn't say that it's insincere, necessarily, but I think he's much more attuned to the public relations value. And he's also more in tune with the times than Hank is, so his proposal for the Caslon tract puts much more emphasis on being environmentally friendly."

"So would you say that this particular project is important to him?" Kaylee asked.

"The thing about Jim is that every project is important. Whatever he's working on at the moment is the most important thing ever. Maybe that's what makes him successful."

"I see," she said. "And what about Roger Findley?"

"If you're wondering who cares the most about this project, Roger would be a strong contender. He's been a contractor for years—I've done a lot of work with him and know him better than the others—but he's only lately started trying to step up and become a developer. Getting the Caslon tract contract would be a big deal for him. I know he wants it badly."

"Based on your knowledge of the men, how do you think each would react to receiving that letter from Emmet Baron?"

Reese shot her a look that indicated he didn't want to speculate.

"Humor me." She smiled. "I won't hold you to anything."

"If you insist." Reese drew in a deep breath and let it out slowly. "Hank probably wouldn't take it too seriously—it's just part of doing business. But he's stubborn enough that he'll be happy to fight it for the sole purpose of making things difficult for Baron."

"Yes, I got that impression," Kaylee said. "DeeDee and I think we heard him arguing with Emmet in the street the day he died."

Reese nodded. "Hank tells it like it is. Or at least like he sees it."

"That's a diplomatic way to put it," Kaylee said. "So how do you think the others would have reacted to the letter?"

"Jim, I think, probably wouldn't think it was the end of the world, but his response is still going to be 'all hands to battle stations,' because that's the way he is. He's going to treat it as a serious threat, no matter what his personal opinion might be."

"Okay. And Roger?"

Reese shrugged. "He doesn't have either the experience or the resources the other two do. I'd imagine that something like that could really shake him."

Kaylee narrowed her eyes. "And what might he do when shaken?"

"Certainly not attack Emmet Baron, if that's what you're thinking. Roger wants something safe, a sure thing. I think his most likely response would be to withdraw."

"And do you think he'll still do that? You're right—that's what he told me he planned to do. But now that Baron is dead, I'm wondering if he's going to change his mind."

As they completed their loop and approached the dog park entrance, Kaylee saw that Sheriff Maddox had parked in the lot and was making his way toward them.

"Kaylee," Eddie called, raising his hand in greeting. "I've been meaning to call you."

Once he was closer, Kaylee asked, "What can I do for you?"

"I wanted to ask what luck you'd had tracing the plants that are mentioned in . . . that letter." He glanced at Reese.

Kaylee was shaking her head. "I'm sorry, but I haven't had any luck at all. The Petal Pushers and I conducted a cursory survey of the property, but we didn't find anything."

"So they're not there," the sheriff said. "Emmet Baron was bluffing?"

"I can't say that," Kaylee replied. "For one thing, even though Shirley Lucas's paintings are incredibly detailed, they're still paintings, not photographs. But more importantly, because I don't know what the plants are, I don't know where they should be in their seasonal cycle, so I wasn't sure what I was searching for. Shirley's drawings could depict those plants as they appear in September, for instance, and they could appear completely different right now. If I could identify the plants, or at least be more certain of their near relatives, I'd have a better idea of what I should have my eye out for at this time of year."

Maddox rubbed his chin. "So you're not able to say definitely whether the plants are there or not?"

Kaylee shook her head, sorry to disappoint the sheriff. "No, but I'm still investigating. I'm reaching out to colleagues to see if they can help with the identification. And I'm going to meet with Justine Lucas and her grandfather, Shirley's ex-husband, to see if they can shed any light on the situation. I'll probably also go back to the Caslon tract and have another look around, just in case. I'm sorry I haven't been more help."

"Of course you've been a help, Kaylee, and I appreciate it. I'd have no idea where to start with that plant situation." Eddie paused. "You used the word 'investigating' just now . . ." There was a warning tone in his voice. "My own investigation has involved talking to the three developers who received those letters."

"I see," Kaylee said with what she hoped was an innocent expression.

"And they all say that they've also heard from you." The sheriff raised an eyebrow.

"I thought perhaps Emmet Baron might have followed up his letter by seeing them in person. And if he did, he might have offered proof of his claims, which might have helped us find something, if there's anything to find. It seemed worth checking."

"I appreciate your thoroughness, Kaylee, but please keep in mind that we're conducting our own investigation. I've asked for your help on just this specific question."

"Yes sir. I'm sorry if I overstepped."

Maddox visibly relaxed. "It's okay. And I am grateful for your efforts. Good luck with your next steps." With a nod, he started toward his cruiser. After a few steps, however, he stopped and eyed three people walking along the street near his car.

"Those are some of the students from DeeDee's writing workshop," Kaylee explained. "The tall woman is Magdalene, and the short one is Jules. And I think the man's name is Zach."

The three writers were clearly engaged in a very animated discussion. Magdalene in particular was gesticulating broadly, and Kaylee could hear her raised voice, though she couldn't make out what the woman was saying.

"Are they talking or fighting?" Reese asked.

"Talking, I think," Kaylee said uncertainly. She grimaced when Magdalene's swinging arm knocked Jules's hat off her head.

The sheriff made to move in their direction, but Magdalene's cry of dismay, her immediate retrieval of the hat, and obviously earnest expression made it clear that it had been an accident.

"That one doesn't know her own strength," Reese said.

With a chuckle, Eddie continued to his car, waving goodbye as he went.

"Your owner will be here for you any minute," Kaylee told Mitzy, not that the little poodle mix had seemed the least bit anxious about her extended playdate with Bear. For forty-eight hours now, they had stopped their play only for brief periods to eat or sleep. Mitzy was a sweet dog, but she and Bear together had been a riotous handful. Kaylee hadn't exactly been counting the minutes—although she was keeping an eye on the clock to make sure she had enough time to meet Justine at the ferry by noon—but when there was a knock at the door of Wildflower Cottage, she greeted Albert with above-average enthusiasm.

It was nothing, however, compared to the excitement with

which Mitzy welcomed him.

The little white dog came tearing in from the back of the house, barking madly and followed closely by Bear. Albert, however, halted in place when he saw her, drew himself up to his full height, and held up one index finger. Mitzy immediately stopped in her tracks and sat silently on her haunches, with only her madly sweeping tail belying her excitement. Bear seemed nonplussed at her sudden change in behavior but decided to follow her example. Kaylee raised an amused eyebrow.

Finally, the attorney clapped his hands and said, "Where's my good girl?" at which Mitzy leaped into his arms and began licking his face. Abandoned on the floor, Bear trotted over to Kaylee.

"Come on in," Kaylee said after giving Bear some scratches behind the ear. She led Albert through the entry and into the kitchen. "I hope your trip went well."

Albert nodded. "It did, and I am very grateful to you for taking care of Mitzy while I was away. She does hate to be boarded, and she seems to have made good friends with Bear." He smiled at the dachshund.

"The two of them have had a grand time," she assured him.

Albert set Mitzy back down on the floor, but instead of running off with Bear, she remained at her owner's side.

"Are you making good progress with Emmet Baron's estate?" Kaylee asked. She hadn't intended to be quite so blunt, but Albert appeared to be in off-duty mode and didn't seem to mind.

"Sadly, no," he said. "I'm afraid it's very complicated. Emmet had a habit of mingling his business and his personal affairs to a shocking extent. I'd had no notion how much. It's going to take a great deal of work to sort them out."

"I have a question pertaining to the estate."

"Yes?"

"You said that the *Orcas Island Triptych* was one of the pieces of art that Emmet owned outright. If that is the case, can it be turned over to Shirley Lucas's family? I know they have been trying to get it back, and Emmet was making it hard for them to buy it."

Albert crossed his arms and nodded, looking at the floor as he thought. "I have a responsibility to the estate, to take an inventory and settle all debts. If we can't locate an heir, I'll give them all due consideration. But it will take time. Months, at least." And though he hadn't seemed to object to the question, he smoothly forestalled any follow-up inquiries by asking, "All set for the holiday?"

"As ready as I can be." Kaylee smiled. "I can't believe the parade is tomorrow."

"Parade floats must bring brisk business for a flower shop, I'd imagine."

Kaylee nodded. "It may not exactly be the Tournament of Roses Parade, but people do like flowers for their floats. We certainly placed a few larger-than-average orders for red, white, and blue varieties from our suppliers."

"And Emmet's young author is to give a reading, I hear? Now that I've started reading his books, I should like to meet him. Well, speak of the devil." He strode toward the kitchen counter, where Kaylee had left the blue dragon figurine Bear had retrieved from the alley next to the gallery. Picking up the dragon to examine it, he said, "Is this one of the Books of the Night dragons?" He turned it about, eyeing it with interest.

"It seems to be. I found it on the ground," Kaylee replied. "I've been meaning to take it into the shop with me in the hopes that its owner might be one of the Griffin Graves fans in town for his reading. DeeDee tells me that the dragons are actually rather rare."

Putnam carefully set the figure back on the counter. "Yes, they are. Emmet had high hopes for these at one point. He invested a fair amount of money in the design and had a few dozen prototypes made, with plans for mass production overseas. But he took them to the big annual toy fair in New York City, and he couldn't get retailers interested in them. It may have been that the books weren't popular enough to merit them yet, but more than that, even people who knew about the books just felt there was a disconnect."

"How so?" Kaylee asked.

Albert gestured toward the dragon. "The shapes, the facial expressions. They're like dragons from a children's cartoon. But the dragons in the Night books are very sophisticated, as you know. Now that the books have become so popular, these have acquired some status as collector's items, but even still that's only with the most ardent fans. For most readers, the disconnect between these and the dragons they envision is just too great. There's even a subculture of fans that like to make fun of them online." He shrugged. "With the right buyer, this little fellow might fetch a pretty good price, but that doesn't mean that there'd be a market for a mass-produced version."

"So, Baron got lucky again? The limited supply of his prototypes drives up the demand and the price?"

Albert chuckled. "He might have been lucky, if he'd been patient. But after his failure in New York, he just wanted to get rid of them. I recall he peddled them around to various retailers in the Pacific Northwest, and when that didn't work, I believe he even gave some away to booksellers to encourage orders." He shook his head. "And then they started showing up on online auction sites. Emmet was furious."

Kaylee frowned. "It seems like kind of an elementary mistake. Did he even read the books?"

"Emmet was very lucky with the Night books, but that doesn't mean he understands the market. As far as he was concerned, dragons are dragons, and I'm sure his only interest in the design was getting it for as little money as possible."

"I wonder how Griffin feels about that," Kaylee said, half to herself.

Albert continued. "It's booksellers and fans on the Internet who have made those books so successful. Honestly, the whole Night series phenomenon has happened more in spite of Emmet than because of him."

A short while later, Albert packed up Mitzy's gear and left, and as she closed the door after the attorney, a fresh theory sparked in Kaylee's mind. Had someone believed the Books of the Night would do better without Emmet Baron? And had they taken drastic action to make it happen?

15

Justine texted Kaylee to let her know she was already in line to board the ferry, so Kaylee parked quickly when she reached the terminal. She grabbed Bear and her tote, then made her way to the row of cars waiting to embark. She quickly found Justine's midsize SUV and waved as she approached.

"Perfect timing," Justine said as Kaylee climbed into the passenger seat. "The attendant is starting to wave cars on board."

Soon, they had parked on the boat and were able to get out and stretch their legs. The sky was clear and the waters calm, so Kaylee let Bear walk around with her on the leash.

"We could grab a sandwich here on the boat," Justine said as they walked the upper deck. "With this new high-speed service, though, we'll arrive in time for a late lunch at Grandpa's. He's a great cook, and always has roasted pork on hand for sandwiches."

Just then, the boat picked up speed and Kaylee's stomach lurched. "Maybe just a ginger ale," she said, glancing toward the boat's concession stand.

Justine held out her palm. "You get settled here. I'll grab us some drinks."

Kaylee found an open table where she and Justine could face one another and still gaze out at the water. Bear dutifully lay down next to her feet, and Justine joined her shortly with drinks in hand.

After a few sips of the ginger ale, Kaylee felt her stomach settle as she grew accustomed to the motion. "This is the first time I've tried the new service. It might take a little getting used to."

Justine laughed, and the wind sent strands of her dark hair flying. "It's been a lifesaver for me this summer. What with the exhibit and all, I've taken this trip more times in the past few months than I had in years. I'm very glad to be able to save some time."

"You mentioned before that your parents had grown up on the Makah reservation. Do they still live there?" Kaylee asked.

Justine looked down at her hands cradling her drink and shook her head. "They both died young. My dad had a heart attack when he was in his forties, while I was in high school. My mother passed a few years later when the flu turned into pneumonia."

"I'm so sorry," Kaylee said gently.

Justine took a breath and shifted gears. "Our family moved away from the reservation when Darren and I were kids. My father worked construction, so he had to follow the jobs, which were mostly around Seattle. My grandparents were already living outside of Dungeness, just a few hours from the city."

"That's south of the San Juan Islands, isn't it?"

"Yep, right across the sound," Justine said, pointing across the blue expanse of water that lay between them and their destination. "They'd take the ferry over to Orcas Island whenever they got a chance."

"Is that what sparked your grandmother's connection to the island?" Kaylee asked. "She painted it so beautifully in the triptych, I was surprised to hear she'd never lived there."

"She never lived there, but I think she wanted to. She loved the island and said it felt magical to her. Verdant and yet strange. She said once in an interview that Orcas Island seemed like a place where prehistoric animals might still live."

Kaylee laughed along with Justine, but she felt a twinge of anticipation. *Maybe prehistoric plants still thrive in their original forms on the island.*

"Anyway, she was happy in her own home, where she lived

for decades," Justine continued. "After Darren and I grew up, we still all came together for holidays at Shirley's house. That's what we always called it. Grandpa lives there now, though the house was left to Darren and me. I think Darren would do better if he moved back to Dungeness, but he loves his job on the service boat, and he loves Orcas Island."

"What does the service boat do?"

Justine nodded. "It's like a floating grocery store. It takes provisions out to fishing rigs at sea. Darren's been selling his roast pork sandwiches through the service boat. He loves food, and he loves being at sea. It's a good job for him."

"And he's doing okay now?"

"I think the time he spent in custody did him good. He really did need to calm down. That's the thing: Darren bottles up his anger, then it erupts and he rages for a few days. He's not violent, but he gets loud and brash. That's what the police saw." Justine's expression darkened. "The fact that the police won't let him leave the island means he can't work, and I'm worried he'll start to get a little stir-crazy. I don't suppose you have any insights as to what really happened that night?"

Kaylee sighed. "I wish I did. It seems a lot of people felt ill-used by Emmet Baron." Kaylee didn't want to bring up Emmet's crude attempt to extort money from the developers. It wasn't public knowledge yet, and she didn't want to give Justine false hope that someone else out there had a real motive to harm Emmet. Instead, she tried to change the subject. "Are you fluent in Makah?" she asked.

Justine laughed. "Not by a long shot. My vocabulary is limited. We do have a lexicographer on our team, though, and his work is fascinating."

The sound of the motor dropped to a fraction of what it had been. "Ladies and gentlemen, this is the captain," boomed a voice over the intercom. "We're slowing down for a moment while we pass a pod of orca whales off the starboard side. Once we are safely past them, we will resume our regular speed."

Justine and Kaylee, with Bear trotting along behind them, joined the crowd gazing westward. Kaylee wished she'd thought to bring binoculars. For a few moments, she couldn't see anything but sun-dappled waves. Then, a massive black-and-white whale took a flying leap out of the water. Kaylee gasped at the majestic creature, and she continued watching the water until the whales were out of sight.

"That's a first for me," Justine said as they returned to their table. "And I've been making this trip regularly all summer."

A short time later, the captain announced that they were approaching the Dungeness port, so Justine, Kaylee, and Bear returned to Justine's SUV and prepared to disembark.

"The ferry made good time," Justine said cheerily. "We'll be to Shirley's house in about twenty minutes. I hope you're hungry."

Kaylee's stomach rumbled as if on cue. She laughed. "If your grandpa's pork is anything like Darren's, I could eat three sandwiches."

When they arrived at their destination, Justine pointed through the windshield. "There's Grandpa. His first name is Joe, just so you know and don't feel like you have to call him Grandpa." She chuckled.

Shirley's house, as Kaylee herself had come to refer to it mentally, was a wide, yellow bungalow with a white wraparound porch. Joe Lucas sat in a rocking chair on the porch, a long-haired white cat on his lap. Justine scampered out of the car, followed by Kaylee, who had Bear in her arms. Seeing the dog, the cat scrambled through an open window into the house.

"There's my girl!" Joe pushed himself out of the chair and ambled down the steps to Justine, a subtle limp in his gait. He wrapped her in a bear hug. "It's been way too long, Teeny Bean."

"I know," Justine replied, her voice muffled by his shoulder.

"How are you holding up?" he asked, finally letting go.

Justine sighed. "It's been a week, Grandpa."

"A long week, from the sound of it," he said, winking at Kaylee.

"This is my friend, Kaylee Bleu," Justine said. "She's the plant taxonomist I told you about on the phone. She owns a flower shop, and she is very interested in learning more about Shirley's garden."

"The garden, eh?" Joe repeated with evident pleasure. "I'll be happy to give you a tour and tell you what I know. I'm Joe." He and Kaylee shook hands, then he extended his hand toward Bear. "And who is this handsome fellow?" The dog sniffed Joe's fingers and then licked merrily, his tail slapping against Kaylee's side.

"This is Bear," Kaylee answered.

"Nice to meet you, Bear." Joe gave the dachshund a scratch under the chin, which Bear leaned into, nearly tumbling out of Kaylee's arms. "I hope you girls haven't eaten yet."

"No sir," Kaylee said.

He laughed. "It's just Joe. 'Sir' is for old people."

He ushered them into the house and through it. Inside, worn wooden floors and unfussy white walls served as a neutral backdrop for artwork after artwork. Framed paintings and drawings of all shapes and sizes crowded the walls from knee level to ceiling. Kaylee recognized many as Shirley's by her signature style, but some, such as the charcoal portraits, seemed as though they might be the work of someone else.

Glass doors at the back of the house opened to a large backyard that was bordered all the way around by tall hedges. Stepping through the doors onto a tile walkway, Kaylee caught the scent of roast pork. "That smells amazing," she said.

Justine sniffed the air theatrically. "Grandpa, please tell us that's for *our* lunch."

"That's right, and for dinner, and then lunch again and dinner, and—"

"Lucky us," Justine interrupted.

Joe chucked her under the chin, then led the way to a patio. "Watch your step, ladies," he warned. "These old terra-cotta tiles are getting a little raggedy."

Under the shade of a tree, a weathered cedar picnic table was festooned with bright yellow and orange place mats, set with paper plates in wicker holders and tall amber-tinted glasses. In the center of the table was a sweating jug of iced tea, a platter of barbecued pork, a bowl of coleslaw with plastic wrap over it, and a large platter of buns covered with a dish towel. It reminded Kaylee of a picture she had of her grandparents at a similar table in the 1960s.

Kaylee realized then that she'd been craving the pulled pork sandwiches since the night of the reception. They all settled in their chairs and Bear curled up obediently at Kaylee's feet, watching carefully to make sure she didn't drop any delicious tidbits. They sat down and dug in.

At first bite, Kaylee nearly swooned. Once she'd washed it down with some tea, she said, "Joe, this is incredible. I thought Darren's barbecued pork was the best I'd ever had, but I might have been wrong."

"Ah, he comes by his talent honestly," Joe said. "And speaking of him, Justine, how is that brother of yours doing?"

"He's fine, Grandpa, really." Justine laid a reassuring hand on her grandfather's forearm. "It's going to work out. But having you there will help keep him on an even keel in the meantime."

Joe nodded, then turned his gaze to Kaylee. A hard gleam had come into his eye. "That Emmet Baron. It's true he bought a lot of my wife's paintings. At first, at least, we were glad of it. Not so much for the money, but for the recognition. It was a long time coming. But in the end, it turned out he wasn't a friend to us at all."

"He was no friend to anybody," Justine muttered.

Joe sat back and surveyed the garden. "He was a customer, but he had his own interests to look out for, and I can respect that. He got greedy, though, and at the expense of my grandchildren." He shook his head. "I can't forgive that. And I can't say I'm sorry the man's dead. He was a crook." He popped the last bite of his sandwich in his mouth.

"Grandpa, I'm not sure talk like that would help Darren." Justine cast an embarrassed glance at Kaylee.

Joe swallowed his food and grinned. "I won't repeat it. Scout's honor." He shifted in his chair so he was facing Kaylee. "Now, young lady. Was there something here you wanted to see?"

Shirley's garden far surpassed Kaylee's expectations. It wasn't large, maybe a quarter of an acre, but it had a rhythm and organization to it that made it at once soothing and invigorating. Like her plant portraits, Shirley's garden featured layer after layer of color, texture, and symbolism. The straw-strewn paths spiraled out from a patch of tall sunflowers in the center. Each patch was shaped like a petal, and each petal contained a mix of vegetables, herbs, grasses, and flowers. The flowering plants were arranged so that each cluster reached its peak just before the next one.

"As the spring and summer progress, the blooms will radiate outward," Justine explained as they explored the space. "That goes until late fall, and then the turning leaves, flowers gone to seed, and bare twigs seem to fold inward to wait out the winter."

"It's truly a masterpiece," Kaylee said appreciatively. "How did Shirley ever conceive of such a thing?"

"All winter long, she would read garden catalogs and make notes about watering, germination periods, plant compatibility," Joe said. "She kept a chart so elaborate I couldn't even begin to decipher it when she first showed it to me."

"And she didn't just do it once. She created a new plan every year." Justine chuckled. "I have one of her charts framed. It's more detailed than a horoscope chart."

"Oh, it includes that too," Joe said. "Shirley put the lunar cycles on the chart."

Justine stopped to deadhead a few flowers. "During the summer, she'd make notes in the chart, little corrections and reminders that would get incorporated into her chart for the next year's garden."

"This is amazing," Kaylee said with true wonder. "I'm impressed that you've managed to duplicate her vision, Joe."

"I haven't," he said. "Not really. This was the last garden she planned. We just replant it and maintain it." He removed his straw hat and wiped his brow with a red bandanna he pulled from his back pocket. "Darren and Justine come and help with the spring planting and putting the garden to bed in the late fall. I just try to keep the weeds at bay and maintain the paths. Shelby, the cat you saw earlier, does his part to scare away the mice and other critters."

Walking along the garden's petal-shaped sections felt meditative to Kaylee, and she reveled in the intoxicating colors and aromas. The question most on her mind, though, concerned the plant depicted in the center panel of the *Orcas Island Triptych*. Kaylee's trained eye spotted some rare specimens, but nothing in the garden resembled that peculiar plant.

"Joe," she said. "I've become a bit . . . obsessed, I guess, with the plant in the *Orcas Island Triptych*. I spent my academic career studying plants, and yet for the life of me, I can't identify it." She stopped. "I don't know if you're aware of this, but Emmet Baron claimed that Shirley had discovered a rare or possibly extinct species. He says that's what was painted in the triptych. Can you tell me anything about it?"

Joe gazed at Kaylee for a long moment. "I suppose for a fellow gardener, not to mention a professional botanist, Baron's claim might sound like he knew of a secret river of gold."

Kaylee smiled and gave a faint shrug. "It's been nagging at me, I admit."

Joe resumed walking along the path. "I do know a little something about it, as it happens. But I'm sorry to say that I don't think you're going to like it."

Kaylee steeled herself. "Go ahead and tell me, whatever it is."

"The triptych was Shirley's last major work. She used to call it her 'royal beauty.' She was getting mighty fanciful by that time." He let out a mournful sigh. "She said she was stirring up all of her favorite plants into one very extraordinary plant."

Understanding swept over Kaylee and she realized in an instant the answer to her question: The *Orcas Island Triptych* didn't depict a long-lost, extinct, or otherwise rare plant. The only place that plant had ever existed was in Shirley Lucas's imagination.

16

Kaylee absorbed Joe's revelation for a few moments. "All of her favorite plants . . . ," she murmured. "So that's why it's both familiar and strange at the same time." It was a fantasy not unknown to her. What would her ideal plant be? What if she could take her favorite things about her favorite plants and put them all together? For Kaylee, it had only been an idle mental exercise, but Shirley Lucas had been talented enough to turn that daydream into a reality of sorts.

Any sense of disappointment Kaylee had initially felt at learning she wouldn't be discovering an extinct species of plant evaporated when she realized what Shirley had done. "How wonderful to be able to capture your dreams on paper," she said. "Or canvas, I guess."

Joe, who had been watching her a little anxiously, now smiled. "She put everything into that triptych," he said earnestly, "which is one of the reasons why the kids are so eager to get it back. All of Shirley's education, her travels, her desires, and loves are represented in that one piece. If you really study it, you'll find little faces in the clouds, constellations in the veins of the leaves, dragonflies and angels—"

"Or aliens," Justine cut in.

Joe shrugged. "Same thing to Shirley. In the side panels, the meadow contains lines of poetry painted in with the finest paintbrush she could find. She'd done something similar with a previous piece, and she liked it so much that she decided to put it in the triptych. She always called it her magnum opus. It comprised all her favorite techniques and ideas."

"She was an incredible talent," Kaylee said.

"The cancer was already in her when she painted it." Joe's voice grew softer and his face sadder. "And we needed the money for treatment, so of course we sold it. And yes, much as we wish we still had it, the price it fetched at least helped to make her a little more comfortable at the end." Joe cleared his throat, and Kaylee wondered if he was fighting tears. "I only wish we could have done more."

Shelby complained heartily about the carrier he was put in for the trip to Orcas Island. However, as soon as the door was shut and latched and the crate was secured in the trunk of Justine's SUV, he promptly settled down.

"He just likes his drama," Joe said dismissively. "Same thing every time. I don't mind though. Some cats will make a fuss the whole time they're in a carrier. I'd rather have him express his opinion at the beginning and then quiet down like he does."

"He's probably jealous of Bear getting to ride up front," Justine joked as she got into the driver's seat.

"Kaylee, why don't you take the front seat so I can check on this one, if need be," Joe said, gesturing toward Shelby. "It's like driving around inside a house, anyway," he muttered as he climbed into the car.

"Grandpa, I happen to know that Kaylee's car is very similar to mine," Justine said cheerfully as she buckled her seat belt. "So mind what you say." Looking over at Kaylee, she said, "He finds this excessive."

"I meant no offense, Kaylee," Joe said.

"None taken. I don't entirely disagree, but I do find I get enough use out of mine—hauling plants and making deliveries and such—that I feel it's justified."

"Exactly!" Justine exclaimed, giving Kaylee the impression that she and her grandfather had had this conversation more than once.

"But the cost to run this thing has got to be ridiculous," Joe said.

Justine snorted derisively. "It's not like your old rattletraps have exactly been efficient. Yes, this may be bigger, but its efficiency makes it no more expensive to drive than your antiques. It's actually more efficient than those sad old things."

Kaylee shifted in the passenger seat so she could see Joe. "Do you like classic cars?"

"I use the term 'antique' in the loosest possible way," Justine said before Joe could respond. "What I mean is 'junk heaps that nobody else wants.'"

Ignoring her, Joe smiled at Kaylee. "Yes I do."

"Are you good with cars, then? Do you repair them yourself? Fix them up?"

Joe's expression soured a bit when his granddaughter sharply yelped, "Ha!"

"Well, no," he admitted. "I've never been very mechanical."

"He drives them until they fall apart," Justine said, "and then goes out in search of the next. Which is why he happens to be 'between cars' at the moment."

"Not for long," Joe said. "Brownie says he can get me an '86 Datsun that's in good shape."

"Brownie!" Justine cried. "The last car you got from him only lasted six months."

"Considering what I paid for it," Joe said placidly, "that was about right."

Justine snorted. "If only your more sensible character traits had rubbed off on Darren."

"He drives old cars too?" Kaylee asked. "I thought he had a truck. I saw it at the reception." She recalled the exhaust fumes she had smelled that night and felt a growing sense of unease.

"The truck was borrowed," Justine said. "For cars, he takes after Grandpa. Rattletraps all day, every day."

"Maybe Darren would like the Datsun," Joe said thoughtfully.

"What's he driving now?" Kaylee asked, trying to keep the edge out of her voice.

Justine smirked. "Something hardly roadworthy, probably."

"Come on now—just because you want to drive a shiny new tank doesn't mean the rest of us agree," Joe argued.

"How is a Datsun anything but an old tank?"

While grandfather and granddaughter continued to banter, Kaylee tried to fight her growing suspicions. Had Darren returned to the gallery in one of his "rattletraps" the night of Emmet's death? She shivered. The implications of that were something she didn't particularly want to ponder.

By the time Kaylee returned to Turtle Cove, it was almost time for that evening's Petal Pushers meeting. Although the group usually met on Tuesdays, they'd shifted their meeting to Sunday night since Mary and Herb were traveling to British Columbia on vacation and were leaving Tuesday morning. Without time to run home—and nothing in her refrigerator to serve her friends anyway—she drove straight from the ferry terminal to the Pacific Street Diner to pick up a snack offering for the meeting. Small towns were wonderful, but one of the drawbacks was that almost everything was closed by six o'clock on Sunday evening, if they were open that day at all. Thankfully, the diner was open later, and Kaylee knew they'd have a display case full of delicious pies.

Stepping into the restaurant, Kaylee spotted Gretchen Cooper at the front counter. Gretchen worked part-time for Jessica at Death by Chocolate, and she picked up weekend hours at the diner as well. Before she could greet Gretchen, however, Kaylee's attention was drawn to a noisy group of patrons talking animatedly around two small tables that had been pushed together. She recognized all six participants from the writing workshop.

"Has this become the after-class hangout?" Kaylee asked Gretchen as she approached the front counter with a nod toward the group.

"They came for lunch, and now post-workshop coffee, and they look like they plan to stay all night. And the things they're talking about!" Gretchen pulled a face. "I guess I should read the books to understand, but they sound pretty weird."

"I felt that way at first," Kaylee admitted. "I'm not big into fantasy. But if you enjoy mysteries at all, you'll like this series."

"Maybe," Gretchen said, sounding unconvinced. "Would you like a table for dinner?"

"No thanks." Kaylee was still full from the delicious lunch Joe had served. "I was just hoping to pick up a pie if you have any left."

Gretchen bent to view the display case. "We've got strawberry rhubarb, apple crumble, and key lime."

"Those all sound good. Let's go with the strawberry rhubarb."

As Kaylee waited for Gretchen to box up her selection, she heard a familiar voice call out, "Katie! Katie! We need you."

She glanced toward the dining area to see that Jules was gesturing to her and some of the writers were watching her expectantly. Others had their eyes cast down, and Kaylee sensed a degree of tension emanating from the group.

"Me?" She pointed to herself, and Jules nodded.

"Did I get your name wrong?" Jules asked nervously as Kaylee approached the table.

Deciding to ignore the group's unease, Kaylee corrected her with amusement. "It's Kaylee, actually. What can I do for you?"

"We need your expert opinion," Rita, the older student, said. "We're having an argument about Griffin's twin planets, Ellaryn and Netiril, and what life-forms could grow on them."

"Okay." Kaylee recalled that, in the universe of the books, these twin planets revolved around each other and their sun, and their inhabitants migrated between them in an intertwined story line.

Rita gestured toward one of the young men. "Jamie here says that the colonies couldn't survive the winters."

"The science has got to be plausible," Jamie insisted in a somewhat petulant tone. "At the aphelion of their solar orbit—"

"Jamie," Zach said sharply.

Jamie sighed theatrically. In a tone bordering on condescension, he said, "At the point in their elliptical orbit when they are farthest from the star, and with the regular occlusion caused by their orbit about one another, neither one would receive enough energy from their sun to support the kind of fantastic vegetation that Griffin describes." He raised an eyebrow triumphantly at Kaylee. "Don't you agree?" It wasn't really a question.

Kaylee had no time to reply before Magdalene hollered, "You insufferable pedant!" She began jabbing a rigid index finger into his chest. "You don't begin to have enough data to make that claim. You don't know their distance from the sun. You don't know the period of their orbit around each other. And you don't even know for sure that they are both exactly in the plane of the ecliptic." She punctuated each point with a jab. "Any of those factors would affect how much sunlight reached the planets. You don't think Griffin hasn't thought of all that?"

By now, Magdalene had half risen out of her seat and was

leaning over Jamie, who sat back in his chair and stared up at her in alarm. The other members of the group were similarly frozen in place.

Finally, Jules said with an awkward laugh, "Wow, Magdalene, tell us how you really feel." The others also forced a chuckle, and Magdalene sat down abruptly. Kaylee could see Jamie's face reddening ominously, but Jules quickly continued, "Well, Kaylee, you can see how seriously we take this. Any insights to offer as a scientist?"

Kaylee tried to emulate Jules's lighthearted tone. "I'm strictly terrestrial plants. What you need is an astrobotanist."

"Exobotanist," Jamie muttered, but the others were all gamely chuckling again, clearly eager to put the incident behind them.

"Sorry," Magdalene said. "I got carried away."

Jamie hesitated, then nodded acceptance of the apology.

Kaylee waited a beat and then said brightly, "Well, I'll leave you to it then." But her stomach sank as she left. This workshop had been so important to DeeDee. Was it destined to flounder so close to the end on personality clashes? What would Griffin think? It even occurred to Kaylee, though she berated herself for the thought, that it was a good thing Emmet Baron wasn't around to stir up even more trouble.

Given what she'd observed, Kaylee wondered what the dynamics were like during the workshop itself. She hoped they were on their best behavior in front of their beloved writer. And yet, if they weren't getting along, why were they all out socializing together after hours?

She returned to the front counter, where Gretchen was waiting to ring her up. "Sorry about that." Kaylee lowered her voice. "Speaking of weird."

Gretchen shrugged nonchalantly as she rang up the pie. "I'd be more concerned if I hadn't watched them go through several cycles already. It's true that they're a little excitable—especially that tall woman—but in five minutes, they'll all be friends again."

And sure enough, as Kaylee left the shop, she heard a roar of delighted, genuine laughter from the group.

17

"It was, I don't know, almost protective. Like a mother bear and her cub." Kaylee was describing the incident at the diner to DeeDee while they awaited their fellow Petal Pushers at the Old Cape Lighthouse keeper's quarters where they held their meetings. "It was like she wouldn't hear any criticism of Griffin or the world he has created."

DeeDee nodded but did not seem unduly perturbed. "Yes, they're all what you might call super fans. And Phyl—er, Magdalene is perhaps the most extreme of the lot. But it also binds them together. So far, they've been able to keep any little disagreements under control. And in terms of their own writing efforts, they've all been surprisingly supportive of one another, none more so than her."

"What are you two so deep in conversation about?" Mary asked as she entered with Jessica close behind. Both carried covered trays that they set on a small table along with Kaylee's pie and some finger sandwiches DeeDee had brought. Bear was napping under the table, worn out from his busy days of playing with Mitzy and traveling to Dungeness.

"Just the writing workshop," DeeDee said. "Hosting it has been quite the experience. And we've even had a handful of people stop by, trying to catch sight of the illustrious Griffin Graves."

"As long as they bought something while they were there," Jessica said with a wink. "I'm glad it's going well."

DeeDee chuckled. "Thanks. I can't say there haven't been a few bumps in the road. There was one moment, for instance, when

Griffin was having the students each read aloud what they'd just written for an exercise, and one of them got so worked up that she made this expansive gesture and nearly caught one of my customers right across the nose." She concluded solemnly, "I'm afraid that woman left without buying anything."

As the others laughed, Jessica said, "That's okay, I think she came to my place and bought a croissant to make herself feel better. She told me all about it. So it turns out your workshop is helping other businesses in town too."

"Speaking of croissants, let's dish up some desserts," Mary said, surveying the snack table. "Who made that yummy-looking pie?"

"Somebody at the Pacific Street Diner," Kaylee said. "I had to stop and pick it up on my way because I was gone all day."

"Is that their strawberry rhubarb?" Jessica asked, glancing at the pie as she uncovered her own platter of miniature chocolate tarts. "The diner makes the best I've ever tasted."

Kaylee smiled. "Well that makes me feel better about not bringing something I baked. Mary, are those homemade pretzels?"

"You bet. What's the latest with the Emmet Baron situation?" Mary asked as she put one of DeeDee's finger sandwiches on her plate. "How is Griffin handling it? It must have been a shock."

"From what he says, he seems to be taking it in stride," DeeDee said. "I don't think they were close." She hesitated and then added, "In fact, I don't think there was any love lost between the two."

"Is he still locked into that contract?" Jessica asked, a note of almost maternal concern in her voice. Kaylee wondered if Jessica had taken a liking to Griffin because he was close in age to her own daughter, Mila. "If this Emmet Baron is dead, then surely the contract is null and void."

DeeDee shook her head. "The contract wouldn't have been with Emmet personally, or so I assume. The contract probably would have been with Puget Press, so whatever happens with it will depend on what happens with the publishing house. And I don't know how closely the company is tangled up with Emmet's estate."

"Well, I wish the police would at least figure out what happened to him," Jessica said.

Everyone's gaze went to Kaylee.

Rather than respond, however, Kaylee changed the subject. "Since we are a garden club, I should probably report that I visited Shirley Lucas's garden over on the mainland today."

The other three burst into exclamations of excitement peppered with eager questions.

Kaylee held up her hands to stem the onslaught. "It was beyond words, but I'll do my best to describe it. Nothing I can say will compare to seeing it in person. Her ex-husband has more or less kept it up as it was when she died, and it is absolutely amazing." With that, she embarked on a detailed description of the extraordinary garden.

While normally all the women would have been hanging on every word, it soon became clear from their faces that they were waiting to hear about one item in particular. Finally, Jessica voiced the question her friends were dying to ask. "But what about the plants in the triptych?" she asked. "Did you learn anything about those? Did she actually have them in her garden?"

"Well," Kaylee said, "we won't need to make any further searches of the Caslon tract."

Her friends quickly registered her serious expression, and their own faces fell.

"She made them up," Kaylee told them. "They never existed."

Kaylee thought about Shirley Lucas's imaginary plant on the drive home that evening. As she'd told her friends when they'd expected her to be disappointed by the news that the triptych plant was imaginary, she found herself in awe of Shirley's ability to concoct something so fanciful in her mind and translate it into a realistic image.

She continued to contemplate the artist's talents as she let Bear roam around the yard at Wildflower Cottage for a few minutes before they went inside. It was close enough to bedtime that she wouldn't have to let him out again, and she knew both of them were ready to turn in.

"Come on, Bear," she called as she fished out her keys. The summertime moths were hurling themselves against the light fixture as she opened the screen door and saw an envelope drop to the ground. Someone must have wedged it in the doorjamb while she was gone.

Kaylee had received notes like this before—some from neighbors, others from less friendly folks—but something about this one gave her an odd feeling. She stooped to pick up the envelope and pulled out the sheet of paper inside.

It took her a moment to process what was written on the paper, but when she did so, her heart turned to ice.

It was a crude sketch of a little dog wearing a bow tie next to a leaf that looked terrifyingly like dieffenbachia.

As if that weren't clear enough, there was also a scrawled message: *BACK OFF.*

18

"So you're saying this is supposed to be Bear?" Sheriff Maddox tapped the piece of paper. "And what is this again?" He pointed to the leaf that had been taped to the note.

"Dieffenbachia," Kaylee said. "It has several . . . unsavory nicknames. And it's toxic."

"It's clearly a threat," Reese muttered. He was leaning against the kitchen wall, fidgeting with the blue dragon he'd grabbed off the counter.

Kaylee agreed and had thought so since the moment she saw the paper. She'd scooped up her dog and bolted into the house, then immediately dialed Jessica.

"Call the police right now," her friend had ordered. "I'll call Reese and send him over to check your locks."

Kaylee suspected that her friend just wanted her to have someone there to comfort her. And the calm, kind handyman had instantly made her feel safe when he'd arrived. He'd gone over the whole house, then kept her company until the sheriff had arrived to take her statement.

"So this would kill a person? Or a dog?" Eddie asked now.

Kaylee hesitated. "That's its reputation, but no. Its toxicity is exaggerated. If you chewed that up and swallowed it, your mouth and tongue would swell and be painful, and you probably wouldn't feel too great. It'll definitely make you sick, but it's not likely to kill, though a dog might die from a large dose. People think that it's more poisonous than it actually is."

"I see." The sheriff jotted down some notes. "But this idea

that it's poisonous, that's pretty common?"

"Yes, I'd say so."

"And what about the message?"

"Seems to me it's warning her to back off from her investigation," Reese said as he set down the dragon and started to pace.

Eddie sighed. "You're not really supposed to be conducting an *investigation*, Kaylee. We talked about this. What have you been up to now?"

"Nothing!" Kaylee felt her cheeks redden. "I mean, I already told you that I'd talked to the developers."

"And what about since then, Kaylee?" the sheriff asked.

"Like you asked me to, I've been trying to find out what I could about the plants depicted in Shirley Lucas's triptych."

"I asked you to do some research," Eddie said calmly, "not investigate to the extent that someone sends you threatening notes."

"I haven't done anything to merit this. I was at a dead end with my research until Justine Lucas took me out to Dungeness to meet her grandfather. He showed me Shirley's garden and we talked a bit."

"Do you think there's any chance that this note could be related to that?" he asked.

Kaylee frowned. "I don't see how. It turns out that the plants in the triptych aren't even real. Shirley Lucas made them up. They don't exist and they never did—at the Caslon tract or anywhere else."

Kaylee was not normally given to tears, but between the day's events and her concern for Bear, she felt closer than usual.

If Maddox noticed this, he didn't remark on it. Instead, he merely said, "I see."

Reese stopped his pacing and groaned. "That means that Emmet Baron's threat to the developers was just a bluff."

"Perhaps, but they had no way of knowing that," Eddie

said. "I take it the two of you have been discussing this, then?"

"Reese gave me some insights into the three developers," Kaylee said, sorry to have dragged her friend into what could quickly become an interrogation.

Eddie sighed. "All right, Reese. Why don't you tell me whatever it is that you've told Kaylee?"

Reese quickly summarized all of the information that he had previously shared with Kaylee. Then, with a glance her way, he said, "I've been asking around since Kaylee and I talked, trying to get a sense of how competitive each bid is. What I've learned pretty much confirms what I thought before. Liebling's plan is too traditional, and Findley is considered too unproven. Jim Park seems to be in the 'just right' zone in terms of both the design itself and the experience he brings to the project. The thinking seems to be that he's the most likely to win the contract."

"Meaning that he's the one who has the most to lose from Baron's threat?" Maddox asked.

"Maybe," Reese said slowly. "Then there's also the nature of the project."

The sheriff fixed a sharp eye on Reese. "Meaning what?"

"Of the three, Jim's proposal is the one that most strongly insists on environmentally friendly design elements. But in some ways, that also means that he is the most vulnerable to the particular kind of threat that Baron was making, right?"

"Because that was all about endangering the habitat of an alleged rare or extinct species," Kaylee added.

"Right," Reese said. "So if that went public, it would hurt Jim with his eco-conscious supporters. They'd expect him to walk the walk. I mean, why do you think he makes such a big deal of his electric car?"

The sheriff was nodding slowly. "So Jim Park seems to have the most to lose—both because he appears most likely to get the contract, but also because of the support it would cost him. But tell me, Reese, does he seem to you like the kind of guy who would do something like this?" He gestured toward the note, which he had set down on the table.

Reese frowned. "Well, no, to tell you the truth. Jim Park is nothing if not deliberate. He's the kind of guy who thinks through all the angles. He's going to minimize his risk any way he can. This note seems impulsive, not well-thought-out. I mean, of course Kaylee is going to call the police when she gets something like this. And everyone knows that she already has a good relationship with you, so you're going to take it seriously, and you'll make sure they're caught. I'm surprised that anyone would do this. There's just too many ways that it can backfire. And that's not Jim Park's MO."

Eddie's expression suggested that he agreed with all of this, though he said nothing. Instead, he turned back to Kaylee. "Do you have any thoughts on who might have done this?"

But something else struck Kaylee. "Electric cars," she said.

"Excuse me?" the sheriff said.

"Reese said something about an electric car," she explained, "and it got me thinking about something. Or actually, remembering something."

"Pertaining to this?"

"Pertaining to the night that Emmet Baron died. I'm sorry, I don't think I remembered to tell you this before, but that night, as Jessica and I were leaving the reception, there was a very strong exhaust smell in the area. When I was a girl, exhaust fumes were something you smelled all the time, so you didn't really notice them, and now you just don't seem to smell those fumes as much anymore. I suppose that's a sign of progress—more efficient cars and all that. But it also means that when you do smell it, it sticks out more. You notice it, and you remember it."

"That's good." Eddie was writing in his notebook. "Exhaust fumes. That's something we can ask other witnesses about. See if anyone else noticed, and if so, maybe pin down the time or even the source. Thank you, Kaylee."

"Would you know it if you smelled it again?" Reese asked.

"I don't know. Maybe," Kaylee said. "I have to say, it did seem very distinctive."

Maddox nodded. "Now, do you have any ideas who might have been behind this note?"

"I wish I did," Kaylee said regretfully.

The sheriff got up to leave. "Okay. I'll look into this. But don't forget, tomorrow is the Fourth," he said as Kaylee walked him to the door. "My whole department is going to be tied up with the parade and everything else. I can't promise immediate results."

"I understand," Kaylee said. "I have every confidence you'll do your best."

"Good night then." The sheriff ducked out through the front door, and Kaylee stayed there for a moment watching him walk to his cruiser.

"Jessica thought I should double-check all of your locks," Reese said, joining her.

Kaylee smirked. "She probably thought you should camp out in your truck on the front lawn too."

"She may have mentioned that idea. I will if you want me to." Reese gave her a big grin.

"I think checking the locks is more than enough," Kaylee said. "You're free to go."

"Don't be afraid to call if you need anything. I mean it." He said good night and left.

Kaylee slept poorly, consumed with anxiety for Bear. In some ways, she felt that she could better handle a direct threat to herself than one to her beloved dog. *Who threatens a defenseless animal, anyway?* she thought angrily as she tossed and turned.

Although she got out of bed feeling haggard and unrested the next morning, Bear, if anything, seemed more chipper than usual. "Ignorance is bliss," she told him as he followed her to the coffee maker, and he wagged his tail as if in agreement.

Even though it was the Fourth of July, Kaylee had scheduled The Flower Patch to be open for the morning, closing in time for the parade that afternoon. She suspected that some of the parade float builders would be in seeking replacement blooms or additions to their floral displays, and perhaps some early arrivals for the parade would like to browse while they waited for it to start.

As Kaylee ate her breakfast and got dressed, she pondered who could have sent her the note. It had been left at her house, so the person in question knew where she lived—not that it was some big secret in a town as small as Turtle Cove.

Kaylee's plan for later in the day involved attending the parade and then Griffin's reading at Between the Lines, which posed a problem for Bear's safety, since the best way to ensure it was to keep him with her. The parade was going to be outside, of course, and the weather was expected to be hot and humid. Kaylee didn't like the idea of dragging poor Bear around in uncomfortable conditions. Even if she brought him water, there was no guarantee she could find him shade, and he could run the risk of suffering heatstroke. Normally he'd be fine by himself at The Flower Patch, but with this threat, she hesitated to leave him there by himself.

The fact remained that Kaylee wasn't sure how seriously to take the threat. Part of her felt certain that it would prove to be the work of someone whose bark was worse than his bite—the drawing had been crude, after all, and almost childlike. But even if she wanted to believe the note wasn't serious, she had to behave as if the threat was credible. If she didn't and something happened to Bear, how could she live with herself afterward?

One thing at a time, she told herself firmly as she grabbed her tote and put Bear on a leash. Bear would come with her to The Flower Patch, and she'd work out later how to handle the rest of the day. She filled up a travel mug of coffee and, seeing the blue dragon on the counter where Reese had left it the night before, she grabbed it and put it in her bag. Maybe she could ask around at the reading and see if any of the Griffin Graves fans in attendance had lost it. That would at least give her one less thing to worry about.

"Thank you so much, Kaylee," Kathy Fitz gushed. "You're a miracle worker."

"Glad I could help," Kaylee said. "I can't wait to see the Orcas Island Library's float after you get it all fixed up."

"We shouldn't have tried to add the live blooms last night." The librarian shook her head. "They all looked so sad this morning. We're lucky you had so many spare sunflowers. I owe you dinner. Call me."

Kathy dashed off to join the rest of the library staff in reviving their float, leaving Kaylee in a shop that was finally quiet. Kathy's had been the third floral float emergency that Kaylee had resolved that morning, and she hoped that it would be the last, especially since Mary had the day off. Between the lack of sleep and the worry over Bear, her energy reserves were seriously depleted. It wasn't quite noon yet, but Kaylee thought she might be justified in closing up early.

She had just checked that Bear was still safely sleeping on his bed when she heard the door chime yet again. Putting on a brave face, she turned to greet the latest customer, and was surprised to see Albert Putnam and Mitzy walk in.

"Good morning, Ms. Bleu," he said, "and happy Fourth of July." Mitzy, sensing the presence of her friend, struggled out of Albert's arms and bounded around the shop in search of Bear.

"Same to you. Are you in town for the parade?"

Albert frowned. "Actually, I'm trying to get a few errands done in order to get out of town before it starts. I'm afraid that something like a parade is just a little too much stimulation for Mitzy."

Both Mitzy and Bear seemed sufficiently stimulated already, since they were now chasing each other about the shop.

"Oh, I know what you mean," Kaylee said with feeling. "I've been trying to figure out all morning what to do with Bear. But I'm sorry, you're pressed for time. What can I do for you?"

"Well, I was thinking about what you said about Shirley Lucas's triptych. The grandchildren, as I recall, were interested in buying it back, and Emmet was being difficult about it."

"That's right. You said that it would take a long time to sort out."

"Yes, I'm afraid that's still possible," Albert said carefully, "but it may be that I've begun to see a path forward, and I thought I would let you know."

"Oh?" She could use a little good news.

"We discussed how the triptych was a work that Emmet owned outright, and that this differentiated it from many of the others in the house, which he did not own but only had on loan."

"Through Clive Randall," Kaylee added.

Albert nodded confirmation but continued on a somewhat different tack. "I told you that one of the things I'm responsible for is settling the estate's debts, which were considerable."

Kaylee's heart sank again. Surely a valuable work like the triptych was going to need to be sold off for top dollar in order to settle these debts. And that would surely put Justine and

Darren out of the running.

"It turns out," Albert continued, now with a slight twinkle in his eye, "that Emmet's arrangement with the Randall Gallery was not a simple loan of the works. Emmet was supposed to be paying a borrower's fee for each of the works that he did not own outright." He sighed. "Emmet, being Emmet, naturally did not pay it, at least not after the first one or two times. But Mr. Randall was reluctant to press the matter, since Emmet did also have a history of buying, and Mr. Randall hoped that most or all of these loans would eventually turn into purchases."

"What do you mean?"

Albert gave a small smile. "It turns out that the estate is considerably in debt to Mr. Randall. Now, we're still a long way from having any formal agreement, but I have had a preliminary conversation with him. I believe that he could be persuaded to accept the return of the triptych as settlement of the estate's debt. And that he might in turn be willing to sell it back to the grandchildren—for a quite nominal sum—in exchange for the exclusive rights to represent Shirley Lucas's other works to buyers." He paused. "Do you think this is an arrangement that would be acceptable to the grandchildren?"

Kaylee beamed at him. "I think it would be wonderful. May I share it with them?"

"If you would be so kind, but please do emphasize that nothing is set in stone yet. And if it is of interest, please ask them to get in touch with me." He paused, watching Mitzy and Bear, who had settled down side by side. "You said that you were wondering what to do with Bear?"

She nodded. "It's just that I was planning to attend the parade today, and then Griffin Graves's reading at the bookstore. The parade will be too hot, and the reading will be too crowded."

"Then perhaps you would permit me to return your earlier

favor. I could take Bear to the cottage I've rented, where he will avoid the commotion of the parade and whatnot. I'll bring him back to you here this evening."

Kaylee's first reaction was panic. Could Albert be the person who had left the threatening note? Why did he want to get her dog away from her? But she realized quickly that he could have no possible reason for doing so, and besides, given how he treated Mitzy, she couldn't imagine that he would ever threaten a dog. And she realized that if there really was someone out there who wanted to hurt Bear, the last place they would look would be with Albert Putnam.

Though the thought of letting Bear out of her sight made her uneasy, this could be exactly the solution she needed. "You know," she said at last, "if you really wouldn't mind, I would be very grateful."

Albert's face radiated a guileless pleasure, and soon he was walking out the door with Bear and Mitzy prancing beside him. Kaylee was thankful to have Bear's safety ensured, but as she waved goodbye, she still felt prickled by icy needles of dread.

19

Sending Bear off with Albert was a relief in one way—but in another, his absence only exacerbated Kaylee's anxiety. Although her brain was somewhat foggy from lack of sleep, she felt that it was imperative that she determine who exactly was threatening her and her dog. At noon, she flipped the front door sign to *Closed*, and sat quietly in the kitchen for a few minutes with a glass of iced tea, trying to reason her way through the mysteries at hand.

Back off, the note had said. But back off from what? Her most deliberate actions had been to investigate the plants shown in the triptych, which she had done at the request of the police. This had been spurred by Emmet Baron's attempts to blackmail the developers into hiring him as a consultant, using the images of the triptych for leverage. But this had been purely a bluff. The plants had never existed. And whether or not Emmet Baron had known this, he certainly knew that he did not possess any evidence that they were endangered plants, whatever he claimed to the contrary.

Then there was the larger question of the fate of Emmet himself. As far as Kaylee knew, the police still weren't treating his death as a murder. But Baron had certainly been attacked in some way, and whoever committed that attack might be in fear of being charged with murder . . . and be willing to take steps to prevent that. After all, even though Baron's death may have in fact been the result of positional asphyxia, nobody but the attacker knew what his or her intent had been. And if the intent had been murder, that would shape how the person understood everything else that was happening—and how they viewed Kaylee's role in it.

The fact that the police were investigating the death would make the attacker nervous. And Kaylee was known to be helping them, as she'd done many times before. Still, she was hardly central to this case. Why threaten Bear? Emmet's attacker would be unwise to increase the level of police scrutiny into their actions. Wouldn't they do better to simply lie low? Unless, of course, Kaylee was onto some clue that would lead to them. But what could that be?

She sighed in frustration. This was all too speculative. What she needed was something concrete to focus on. The note was concrete, and it was the immediate cause of her distress.

The sheriff, of course, had taken the note with him, but Kaylee had snapped a photo with her phone. She brought up the image and stared at it. The drawing of Bear and the caustic warning had been done in blue ink on plain white paper, a staple of every home and office printer Kaylee had ever come across. The words, in block capitals, didn't appear distinctive enough for identification. The drawing was fairly crude, though whether that was lack of talent or deliberate was impossible to say.

And the dieffenbachia?

Kaylee's brain lit up with a connection she had previously failed to make. It was a dieffenbachia that the workshop students had initially considered buying as a gift for Griffin, until Kaylee made a point of informing them that the leaves might be harmful to pets. The alternative, the pinstripe plant, was going to be presented at the reading later that day. And, Kaylee remembered, there had even been some jokes made about the toxicity of the dieffenbachia. At least one of the students was already aware of its reputation in that area. Who had said something about it? Kaylee couldn't remember.

Dieffenbachia, she thought. *Pretty, shade tolerant, often used indoors.* A good choice for a houseplant and common enough that she'd never given it a second thought. Could it be a coincidence that it was the same plant used in the threatening note?

Kaylee had to admit that a coincidence was possible, even likely. But as a researcher, she believed that any coincidence called for further investigation, and while she could not imagine a reason why any of the workshop participants—or more than one?—would want to send her a threatening note telling her to back off from something, the coincidence of the dieffenbachia gave Kaylee that which she needed above all else: a clear next step that she could pursue.

She would talk to the students and see what she could learn.

Since she had closed early and was far too anxious to be hungry for lunch, Kaylee still had time before the parade started. She knew that the workshop participants had the day off until the time of the reading, in which Griffin had insisted that they all participate. She also knew that several of them were staying at the Tall Pines B&B, so she decided to begin her search there.

Located about a mile outside town limits, the Tall Pines B&B was aptly named, as it was nestled in a thick forest that offered cool shade on that warm summer day. Kaylee found Jules, Zach, and Kent sitting in Adirondack chairs set up around an off-duty fire ring.

"Hey, Kaylee!" Jules called as Kaylee approached. The young writer smiled. "At least I remembered your name this time, right?"

"Hi Jules." Kaylee angled her gaze around Jules and waved at the others. "Hi guys."

"Hey," they said in unison.

"Where's everyone else?" Kaylee asked, trying to sound nonchalant.

"Rita and Jamie went into town," Jules explained.

"What about Magdalene?"

Jules shrugged. "I couldn't say. She's the only one of us not staying here. Besides, she gets worked up when you ask her personal questions."

"Or when you don't share her opinion about literature, or when you breathe wrong," Zach said drily.

"She means well, Zach," Jules chided. "It's not her fault she gets a little excited sometimes."

"Speaking of excited," Kaylee said, "are you guys ready for the reading tonight?"

"Are we ever," Kent said. "Griffin is going to read something nobody has heard yet from one of the upcoming books."

"I'm prepared for my mind to be totally blown." Zach punctuated his statement by making an explosion sound, and everyone laughed.

It occurred to Kaylee that she hadn't prepared an excuse for why she would be seeking these folks out. She couldn't exactly lead with "Did you threaten my dog?" After thinking for a moment, she asked, a little lamely, "Are you still planning to present Griffin with the plant?"

Jules smiled, and Zach and Kent laughed outright. "Oh yes," Jules said, "I'm sure that will still happen."

"Magdalene is completely fixated on it," Kent explained. "It was her idea in the first place, and I suspect that she is at her cottage right now practicing a speech."

Puzzled, Kaylee asked, "So did the rest of you not think it was a good idea?"

Jules, apparently remembering that Kaylee sold plants and

flowers for a living, quickly jumped in. "Oh no, everyone agreed it was a good idea. At least, we are all eager to express our gratitude in some way, and a plant that resembles what might have grown on Griffin's worlds is perfect. It's just that Magdalene has been somewhat more invested in the whole idea than the rest of us. You may have noticed she's very . . . earnest."

Kaylee smiled. "Yes, so I've seen. And how about you three? Now that the workshop is almost over, will you be spending any additional time with us here in Turtle Cove?"

Jules shook her head. "I'm off on the first ferry tomorrow, I'm afraid. I have to get back to my day job."

"Kent and I are planning a hike tomorrow, and then we'll take off the next day," Zach said.

"And some of you came in early, right? DeeDee told me that Conrad had offered a special package for workshop participants here at the Tall Pines."

"That's why I have to get back," Jules said. "I've already been here a week and used up almost all of my vacation time. And these guys arrived the same day I did." She jerked a thumb at Zach and Kent, who nodded.

"What about the others?" Kaylee pressed, straining for a nonchalant tone.

"Let's see," Zach said. "Rita arrived the day after we did. And Magdalene said she had her cottage rented for the week. Or was it two? She was complaining about how inflexible the owners had been. So yes, I guess Jamie was the only one to arrive just in time for the workshop."

"I don't suppose any of you happened to attend the reception on Tuesday that a gallery had for their new exhibit of the work of a local artist?" Her questions all felt rather ham-fisted to Kaylee, but the three young people didn't seem to mind.

"I didn't go to the opening, but I did stop by on Saturday,"

Kent said. "That lady's paintings looked just like what you'd find on Ellaryn."

After a pause, Jules asked, "Isn't the gallery where that man was killed?"

"Yes, Emmet Baron," Kaylee said. "He was Griffin's publisher. Did you know that?" She watched the three exchange glances.

"Yes," Zach finally said. "There was some talk about it. I don't know the details, but we've all gotten the impression that he treated Griffin very shabbily. Not that he deserved to die, of course, but I think we all had less sympathy for him than we might have otherwise. He doesn't seem to have been a pleasant man."

"Magdalene would know all about the publishing deal," Kent added. "At least, she seemed to be fairly knowledgeable about the situation—or as knowledgeable as anyone can be from Internet gossip. And she seemed to think that this Baron guy had totally taken advantage of Griffin."

Jules sat back. "Like I said, she's earnest."

Kaylee bit her lip then asked, "So where is Magdalene staying?"

This provoked a fair amount of discussion, since none of them had been out to the cottage, but each seemed to have notions about where it was. After several long exchanges, they resorted to drawing maps on their ever-present writer's notepads. Sadly, their drawings were all completely different. After further consultation, they finally came to a consensus and drew up a fourth map that they proudly presented to Kaylee as absolutely reliable.

It matched no place on Orcas Island that she was familiar with.

Before she could find the words to thank them, however, Zach glanced at his watch and leaped to his feet. "Of course she won't be there now anyway," he said cheerfully. "We all agreed to meet up at the parade, and it's about to start."

20

Since the young writers had been planning to walk and she had clearly held them up, Kaylee gladly offered them a ride into town. After they parked behind the flower shop, they found Rita, Jamie, and Magdalene already awaiting them at their rendezvous point in front of Between the Lines. Everyone greeted Kaylee warmly before turning their attention to the parade, which had just begun.

The day had turned blazingly hot, and the heat was having a soporific effect on the sleep-deprived Kaylee. In fact, the effort of keeping focused was giving her a headache. After a peek into her tote to look for her water bottle, she realized with disappointment that she'd left it at the shop. *I don't have any water, but at least I have a blue dragon toy,* she thought wryly. She wondered if she should get herself an iced tea or coffee, but she knew the lines at all the cafés would be long. She could run back to The Flower Patch for her water bottle, but she didn't want to miss the parade. She'd be fine until it was over.

Main Street was lined with cheerful crowds in which children waved small American flags. The parade was to come down Main Street toward the ocean, turn right onto Shoreline Drive, and make its way to the end point at the Turtle Cove Town Park.

Turtle Cove, for its small size, boasted three marching bands. Following the color guard—three teenagers in uniform carrying the American flag, the Washington state flag, and the local high school flag—the high school band started off the parade, led by a drum major with a traditional large baton. When the band had marched to a point just beyond where Kaylee was standing, they came to a standstill and started to play a jazzy rendition of "Stars and Stripes Forever."

Kaylee shaded her eyes and searched the crowds for her friends, but there were too many people. The glaring sun reflected off sunglasses and phone screens, making it nearly impossible to see anyone clearly anyway.

A pickup truck pulled the first float, which carried the mayor and town officers. The float was decked with patriotic bunting and several red, white, and blue bouquets from The Flower Patch. As the mayor waved, the town officers tossed candy to children in the crowd.

After the mayor's float came a sleek white electric car with American flags secured to the front headlights and bunting across the trunk. Nearby, Jim Park zigzagged across the street to hand out refrigerator magnets with details about recycling and hazardous waste collection days. Kaylee couldn't imagine walking in a parade with the pavement giving off even more heat.

The next float was sponsored by one of the island's lavender farms and featured pink, blue, and purple stripes of lavender flowers. Kaylee inhaled deeply, enjoying the delicate scent as the float passed by. Even the lavender smelled warm.

When the high school band was out of earshot, the second band emerged. The middle school band was smaller and a little rougher, but not without charm as they played the "Colonel Bogey March." Unlike the formal band uniforms of the high school musicians, these kids were dressed in khaki shorts and matching T-shirts.

A few more floats followed the middle school band, and more candy was tossed out. Then came a slow, crowd-pleasing procession of farm animals—donkeys and cows mostly, none of which were particularly interested in walking as they were supposed to and kept veering off to seek attention and perhaps food among the crowd. A few more floats followed, and then the town band. The ragtag group of retirees brought up the rear with a vivacious rendition of the folk tune "Good Night, Irene."

As the end of the parade passed by, most of the townspeople fell into line behind it in order to follow along to the park. Kaylee's feet hurt, her body felt sunbaked, and her head ached fiercely. She gazed longingly down the street at The Flower Patch, where she could have rested in the dimness of the interior and had something cool to drink. She had just about made up her mind that the Dino-Writes could tell her nothing useful and that she should succumb to the lure of her pleasant shop.

"Why don't we follow along to the park?" Rita suggested. "My car is over that way anyway."

"Would you mind driving us back to the Tall Pines?" Zach asked Rita, who nodded in agreement.

"Are you coming, Magdalene?" Jules asked, putting a hand on the tall woman's arm.

"Nah, I've got to go to my cottage to pick up the plant for Griffin," Magdalene answered. "I didn't want to leave it in the hot car and have it completely withered by the time we gave it to him." She gave a loud laugh at the prospect.

For whatever reason—be it the fact that Magdalene was the only Dino-Write that wasn't staying at the B&B or some other more nebulous cause—Kaylee wanted to ask Magdalene a few questions. "Where are you parked?" she asked before she could stop herself.

"Uh, that way." Magdalene pointed down the alley between The Chic Boutique and Between the Lines that led toward the public sculpture park.

"Great, I'll walk you to your car."

Kaylee and Magdalene said goodbye to the rest of the group,

with assurances that they would all see each other at the reading.

If the young woman was wondering why Kaylee had decided to join her, she didn't ask. Instead, she seemed to be in rather high spirits, talking about the parade and Orcas Island and the beautiful blue waters of Puget Sound in a booming voice, punctuating her comments with her usual expansive gestures.

It was all a bit much for Kaylee's throbbing head, but she managed to ask, "So you've enjoyed your visit? I know some of the others got here early. Did you?" She regretted her bluntness, but it was the best she could do in her overtaxed state.

Magdalene frowned. "I had to arrive last Sunday. The cottage I'm renting only goes by the week strictly starting on Sunday, so I had to take it for two weeks." She brightened a bit. "I figured I'd make a real vacation out of it. I'm glad I've gotten to spend so much time in such a gorgeous place."

"Why didn't you stay at the Tall Pines?" Kaylee knew that Magdalene could be prickly at the best of times, and she sensed that her questions were beginning to provoke the young woman. She was clearly not as laid-back as her fellow Dino-Writes.

After a brief hesitation, Magdalene answered, "I need my space, especially when I'm in unfamiliar surroundings. I can't travel with other people. I tried to go on a cruise once with a cousin of mine, and we almost came to blows. I didn't know how many of the other participants would take the B&B option, but I figured I'd better make my own arrangements. And since all of the others ended up staying there, it's a good thing I did." She shrugged. "If I hadn't had a chance to decompress at the end of the day, this would have been a very different experience. I'd have ended up trying to poison the rest of them or something." This seemed to Kaylee an odd joke to make, but her heart truly froze when Magdalene added brightly, "Thanks to you, I'd have known just how to do it."

"What do you mean?" Kaylee asked sharply.

"That poisonous plant you showed us, remember? Deeferbane or whatever. Turns out there's one of those at the cottage where I'm staying." She frowned and said thoughtfully, "Though of course, if I'd stayed at the B&B, I wouldn't have access to that. But still, I could have gotten it from you, couldn't I?" She smiled at Kaylee. "That's the thing about a writing workshop—everything becomes a plot point. Say, are you okay?"

Kaylee had stopped and was staring at Magdalene in horror. Was there more to this than met the eye? She struggled to focus her thoughts. Did Magdalene intend some subtext with all this talk of poison and dieffenbachia? But if Magdalene had sent the note, why would she be saying all this? To gloat? To reinforce the message? To prove that she had the means and the intent? But why on earth would she . . .

"Did you threaten my dog?" Kaylee blurted. Simultaneously she felt regret, aware that she wasn't thinking straight, but also relief to finally be taking some action—any action—about the threat that had been made to Bear. She was unable to stop herself from continuing, "How could you threaten a defenseless animal?"

Now it was Magdalene's turn to look horrified. At first she simply stared, and then her mouth began to move without making sound. Finally she choked out, "What?"

"My dog is precious to me," Kaylee said, her voice stringent and trembling with emotion. It was unlike Kaylee to shout, let alone to make a scene in public, and part of her was aware that she was in danger of losing control altogether. She felt dizzy and couldn't tell if the cause was emotional or physical. In an only slightly firmer tone, she said, "And to threaten him . . ." She could feel herself becoming uncharacteristically incoherent. "I got a note," she choked out, "with a drawing of Bear on it. And a leaf of dieffenbachia!"

She struggled to draw herself up and glare accusingly at Magdalene.

Magdalene was slowly backing away, her expression crumpling as though she was on the verge of tears. "Threaten? You can't—you can't—" She spun and fled.

And that was the last thing Kaylee saw before she blacked out.

21

"**K**aylee?" Jessica's voice seemed very far away. "Kaylee, can you hear me?" The sound grew a little louder, and Kaylee felt Jessica shake her by the arm. "That's it, I'm calling an ambulance."

Finally forcing herself from the darkness, Kaylee opened one eye. "No don't." She opened her other eye and realized she was on the ground, lying on her side with pebbles digging into the arm pinned beneath her. "I'm fine."

"You most certainly are not," Jessica said.

Kaylee struggled to sit up and then, as if to prove a point, to stand. "I am. I think the heat just got to me a bit."

"What were you doing back here? I only found you because the parking spaces behind the bakery were all full and I had to leave my car near the sculpture park."

"It's a long story." Kaylee sighed. "Why don't we go back to my shop and I'll tell it—after I turn the air-conditioning down to 60 degrees."

A little while later, they sat in The Flower Patch with the shades drawn. Kaylee was stretched out on one of the couches in the consultation room in front of a fan with her feet up on the arm. Jessica brought a wet cloth to hold against her forehead and kept her water glass full. Kaylee, having just caught Jessica up on her day and her altercation with Magdalene, was slumped and spent, clutching the glass in her hand.

"Are you sure you shouldn't go to the hospital?" Jessica asked. "I think you've suffered heat exhaustion."

"No. I think I mostly feel bad about how my talk with Magdalene went off the rails." Kaylee sighed. "You can just tell that she's a little out of her element around people. The kind of accusation I made would shock anybody, but for her it must have been especially upsetting. I should have gone about it differently."

"You're the one who was threatened," Jessica replied. "It seems to me that you're the one who deserves special consideration, not her. Not anyone who threatens an animal."

Kaylee frowned. "I can't convince myself that she was the one who did it, though. I mean, why would she? It doesn't make any sense."

"But you said yourself that she didn't actually deny it," Jessica reminded her.

Kaylee frowned. "I'm not sure that constitutes proof. As I said, she was very upset. And I really wasn't making much sense."

But Jessica, fuming on her friend's behalf, was unwilling to give Magdalene the same benefit of the doubt. "If she didn't deny it, it's as bad as a confession," she said stubbornly.

Kaylee didn't have the mental stamina to argue with that, so they sat for a while in silence.

Finally, Jessica said, "Poor Bear. You were smart to send him somewhere that nobody would suspect."

Kaylee nodded. "I'm glad I didn't have to worry about him getting heat exhaustion too."

Jessica took a deep breath, then asked tentatively, "Kaylee, just how seriously do you think we should take this note?"

Kaylee gazed down at her lap. "I really don't know. Naturally, my first response is emotional, and on that level, every part of me cries that I need to take it very seriously. Intellectually, however, I think it's more bluster than a real threat."

"You can't risk not taking it seriously. I mean, you may believe that the actual threat is small, but if you're wrong, the consequences would be enormous."

Kaylee nodded. This had been her own reasoning as well.

"But then," Jessica continued, "the question becomes how long you take it seriously. I mean, Bear can't stay with Albert Putnam forever. Or even longer than today. How long can you let your life, your behavior be dictated by this threat?"

Kaylee frowned. In her earlier urgency to be "doing something," she hadn't thought beyond the immediate moment. But Jessica had a point. What was the long-term solution? In her weakened state, the problem felt almost insurmountable.

"Any word from the sheriff?" Jessica asked.

Recalling Maddox's words the night before, Kaylee said, "Well, this is a pretty busy day for them already."

"I say we drive out to the sheriff's office and ask Eddie what progress he's making."

"He's probably here in town," Kaylee suggested.

Jessica shook her head. "He was in to get some coffee not too long before I closed for the day—and don't make me remind you how lucky it was that I closed when I did and found you. Anyway, he said that since the parade was over, he was heading back to his office to make some calls."

"Okay, but why don't we just call him?" Kaylee gestured toward the shop's phone.

"Because my car has air-conditioning. And I think a ride might do you good."

On the drive to the sheriff's office in Eastsound, Jessica continued to press the case that Magdalene must have been the one to send the note. "I mean, come on. She just happened to bring up dieffenbachia out of nowhere? Please. And she never actually denied it, remember. This visit will be good. We'll get an update, and we can tell Eddie about this lead."

Kaylee remained doubtful about Jessica's theory, but she agreed that there was no reason not to share the story of her encounter with the sheriff.

When Aida Friedman, the department receptionist, saw them enter, her first comment was, "No Bear?" She was a big fan of the bow-tied canine. But she must have heard about the threat that had been made because she immediately said, "Oh right," and then picked up the phone. "I'll tell the sheriff you're here."

Aside from Aida, the office seemed deserted, and Kaylee assumed that all of the deputies were deployed in town to help handle the crowds. She checked her watch and said, "Jess, we may be late for the reading."

Jessica shrugged. "This is more important." After a beat, she added, "Are you sure you still want to go?"

"Of course," Kaylee said just as Eddie Maddox emerged from his office and waved them in.

Once they were seated, Jessica plunged in before the sheriff could say anything. "Eddie, we think we know who wrote that note to Kaylee."

Maddox sat back in surprise and glanced from one woman to the other, seemingly suppressing a grin. "Oh?"

Kaylee started to demur, but Jessica plowed ahead. "We think it was one of those people in DeeDee's workshop. That big woman, Magdalene, the one who's always loud and waving her arms."

Now a puzzled frown drew the sheriff's eyebrows together. "I see. Why?"

"Tell him, Kaylee," Jessica urged.

Kaylee told him about her day, both about visiting the other writers and then about her encounter with Magdalene that ended in a fainting spell. "The thing is, I appreciate Jess's points, but I'm not as sure that Magdalene sent the note as she is."

Eddie gazed at her with concern. "First of all, Kaylee, how do you feel? Are you sure you shouldn't go to the hospital?"

"I've already tried talking her into it, Eddie," Jessica said drily. "She's not budging."

"I'm fine," Kaylee assured them. "I'm much more concerned about what Magdalene would want me to back off from. I can't figure it out. And since I can't guess what her motive might be, I'm not at all sure that she's the one who sent the note."

The sheriff leaned forward. "There's a good reason for that, Kaylee. She's not the one who sent you the note."

Kaylee smiled wanly, relief flooding her. "So you know who did."

"I do," the sheriff said. "Roger Findley."

Kaylee and Jessica shared a look and then turned back to the sheriff. "What?" Kaylee asked. "Why?"

"As soon as the parade was over, I came back here to call the three developers and make appointments to talk with them." Maddox shrugged. "It was a place to start. But when I called Roger, I'd hardly said who I was before he broke down sobbing on the other end of the line and made a full confession. He'd spent the night consumed with guilt."

"But why would he do it?" Jessica asked.

Eddie reached up and scratched his cheek lightly. "This Caslon development is a big deal for him. He sees it as his chance to step up to a new kind of business. And the thing is, it's already not going well for him. Most people think he's not going to win the job."

"That's what Reese told me too," Kaylee said.

The sheriff continued, "And he'd taken Emmet Baron's threat very seriously, in part, I think, from his lack of experience in these matters. But whatever the reason, when he heard about Baron's death, that was a big relief to him. So when Kaylee started asking about the same thing, he panicked."

"It doesn't seem like he really thought it through," Kaylee observed.

Maddox's brow furrowed. "The thing is, Kaylee, you're going to have to decide whether you want to press charges. Making a threat like that, no matter how poorly thought through, is against the law."

Kaylee's shoulders sagged. She hadn't considered this.

"Roger told me that he's writing you a letter to apologize and explain himself," the sheriff said. "You can wait and make your decision after you read it, if you like. What he may not tell you—and I don't say this to excuse him in any way—is that he's been under a lot of strain lately because his wife was diagnosed with cancer. It's not my place to say more, but the pressure of the whole situation impaired his judgment. Winning that contract would help considerably with medical costs." He spread his hands on his desk. "It's entirely your decision, of course. But for what it's worth, his remorse for his behavior is genuine."

"Thank you. I'm glad to know that." Kaylee frowned in thought. "You said that Findley felt relief at the death of Emmet Baron. What if he was Emmet's attacker?"

The sheriff was already shaking his head before she even finished the question. "We checked into Roger Findley's whereabouts on the night in question. He wasn't even in Turtle Cove."

"So you're still investigating Baron's death? Is it murder after all?" Jessica asked.

"It has not been ruled so," Eddie said with an air of finality.

"But somebody attacked him," Kaylee said, despite Maddox's frown. "Even if he wasn't technically murdered, somebody out there has to answer for that."

22

Eager to make it to Griffin's reading, Kaylee and Jessica left the sheriff's department a short while later—with no charges filed against Roger Findley—and returned to Turtle Cove to find a very crowded Between the Lines.

DeeDee was already standing at a microphone making introductions. Jessica spotted her husband, Luke, across the room and gave Kaylee's arm a gentle squeeze before slipping off to join him. Taking in the crowd, Kaylee saw not only many unfamiliar faces, but also several Turtle Cove residents that she would never have otherwise taken for fans of the mystery-fantasy genre. *They could say the same thing about me, I guess.*

For a young man who seemed shy and ill at ease in person, Griffin appeared very relaxed as he began to address this large group. "I'd like to start by remembering my publisher, Emmet Baron, who recently passed away," Griffin said. "Emmet gave my books a chance before anyone else, and without him, you would all be spending your Independence Day somewhere other than in this fine bookstore." After a few laughs from the crowd, he continued. "And this fine bookstore belongs to the wonderful DeeDee Wilcox, who has generously upended her life for our little workshop this week. I'm not sure she'll invite us back after all of the fuss we caused her, but if she did, we'd be back in a heartbeat."

Kaylee could tell by the faces of those around her that they appreciated the young man's sincerity as much as she did.

"Before we really get going, I'd like to thank the six incredible workshop participants we've had this weekend. I was supposed to come to the island as their instructor, but I believe that they've each taught me far more than I could ever possibly hope to teach them. It has been a great privilege—and a perk of being a best-selling author I hadn't ever given much thought to—to work with you all."

Griffin began clapping his hands, and the rest of the crowd joined in to applaud the six writers, whose faces varied from sheer embarrassment to proudly soaking up the attention.

Once the ovation died down, Griffin concluded his speech. "I've asked each of these fine writers to read a bit of their work, and then I'll force you all to sit through an excerpt from the soon-to-be published *The Night of the Second*, the latest volume in the Books of the Night series."

After another round of applause, Jules stepped forward holding the plant in the cedar box. "Before we really get down to business," she said to the crowd, "we'd like to take the opportunity to present this token of our thanks to you, Griffin. Much like you, it's unassuming at first glance, but if you look more closely, it's full of surprises."

Kaylee chuckled to herself at that, remembering how she'd rigged up the dragons within the leaves of the pinstripe plant.

Once the plant was gifted, each writer took turns reading a short selection from what they'd worked on that week, which went well until it came to Magdalene's turn. Kaylee thought she seemed even more agitated than usual. Worried that her own presence might be upsetting the woman, Kaylee wondered if she should try to make herself more inconspicuous. But after watching Magdalene for a few moments, she guessed that the young woman had not even seen her.

Nevertheless, once at the microphone, it seemed that Magdalene couldn't begin. Griffin stepped up, touched her lightly on the shoulder, and said something in her ear.

With that, she relaxed enough to read her short piece, blushing furiously at the applause when she sat down.

Then Griffin approached the microphone for his own reading. "Before I begin, I've been informed that I'm allowed to share some news with you all. There has been some speculation since Emmet Baron's death about the fate of the Night books." He paused again while the crowd muttered among themselves. "My agent has told me just today that I can legally continue the series with a new publisher." The audience responded with a round of applause, then he continued. "And a deal for a television series based on the books was finalized just this weekend while I've been in Turtle Cove. Production is scheduled to begin later in the year."

This was followed by another round of thunderous applause.

Griffin held up the sheaf of papers in his hand. "I have one more tidbit to share with you all as thanks for being here tonight. A major new character will be introduced in the upcoming book, and the selection I read today is the character's debut scene. Please enjoy this excerpt from *The Night of the Second*."

It was only afterward that Kaylee was able to appreciate just how spellbound the room became when Griffin read to them. At the time, she herself was so caught up in the experience that she didn't even notice how enraptured everyone else was as well. But when the reading ended, and the entire crowd seemed to draw a collective breath as if coming out of a trance before breaking into applause, she had a sense of just how transported they had all been.

Magdalene, she noticed, was quietly weeping.

During the reception afterward, Griffin signed books, the Dino-Writes were congratulated by members of the audience, and Kaylee led Reese into a quiet spot so she could tell him about the resolution of the threatening note. Relief flooded his handsome features. "That's great, Kaylee. Thank you for letting me know." Then his face clouded. "Poor Roger. It's just so unlike him, at least when he's his usual self. I hope his wife is okay."

"Me too," Kaylee agreed.

"I feel like a weight has been lifted. Do you feel better?"

Kaylee smiled a bit at his enthusiasm. "I am so grateful that Bear was never in any real danger. It sounds like Roger regretted it almost immediately."

"Where is Bear, anyway? At The Flower Patch?"

Kaylee was just opening her mouth to respond when she spotted Magdalene slipping out the door. "Will you excuse me? There's something I have to do."

"Of course," Reese said as she hurried away and out of the bookstore.

Kaylee caught up with Magdalene just as she was climbing into her rusty old hatchback. "Magdalene?" she called. "Can I talk with you for a minute?"

Already half-inside the car, the young woman turned when she heard her name, but when she saw Kaylee, her eyes went wide with terror. She finished climbing in and closed the door.

Kaylee's guilt doubled. Stepping up to the car door, she said, "Please. I just wanted to apologize."

Magdalene hesitated, but then cranked down the window. One part of Kaylee's mind reflected that not many cars these days still had hand-cranked windows. But this was quite an old model, what Justine would have called a rattletrap. She pushed these thoughts aside, though, to focus on what she needed to say.

"I'm so sorry for my behavior earlier. I had no business

accusing you like that. I was worried sick about my dog and not feeling well. But I shouldn't have taken it out on you, and I'm very sorry."

For a long time, Magdalene sat staring forward, unmoving. Finally she asked, "Somebody threatened your dog?"

"Yes, they sent a note. And of course, it had nothing to do with you. I was just terrified for my dog, and I was ready to suspect anyone and everyone. But even still, I shouldn't have behaved the way I did."

Magdalene continued to sit and stare at her steering wheel, and Kaylee noticed that the woman was nervously wringing her hands in her lap. She had assumed that she had been the cause of Magdalene's distress, that her unfair accusation and confrontational manner were still eating at the woman. But perhaps she had been taking too much of the blame. If she'd been right, then this clearing of the air should have relieved Magdalene's distress. And yet Kaylee had the feeling that she was still as upset as ever.

Concerned, Kaylee was on the verge of asking Magdalene what else was troubling her.

But suddenly, Magdalene started up her car while saying to her windshield, "I would never hurt a dog."

And in that moment, Kaylee's nose was assaulted by the smell of exhaust.

And everything fell into place.

23

"Magdalene," Kaylee said with quiet urgency as the woman reached for the shift lever on the steering column, "do you know anything about what happened to Emmet Baron?"

With a stricken face, Magdalene dropped her hands back into her lap. For some time, she simply sat there while tears rolled down her cheeks. Then, after a while, she shut the engine off again.

"People will be coming out soon," Kaylee said gently, gesturing back toward the bookstore. "Shall we find somewhere to talk?"

Without a word, Magdalene climbed out of the car, shut the door, and began to walk.

As she had earlier that day, the tall woman headed down the alley toward the sculpture park. This time, they made it all the way to the park, and Kaylee led them to a bench, where they sat down. The sun was sinking lower in the sky and casting a warm glow on everything its rays touched.

They sat in silence, Magdalene hunched forward with her elbows on her knees. Kaylee was trying to give her the space to begin talking on her own, but Magdalene seemed too lost in her own head.

Finally, Kaylee reached into her tote bag and drew out the blue dragon. She handed it to Magdalene. "This is yours, isn't it?"

This seemed to break the dam, and as her tears flowed again, Magdalene started to speak. "I didn't mean to," she sobbed. "It was an accident."

"Just tell me what happened," Kaylee said soothingly. When Magdalene didn't respond, Kaylee prompted her. "You arrived in Turtle Cove on Sunday."

"I wanted to take advantage of being so near the ocean. I live in Spokane, so it's at least half a day's drive to see it. I spent a lot of time out walking along the shore, especially at night. It was so beautiful."

"Did you know Emmet Baron was here?"

Magdalene nodded, but quickly added, "But I wasn't planning anything. I just, you know, saw it online."

"He announced his schedule online?"

"Sure. He'd posted on social media about the gallery opening. But it's not like I follow him on the app or anything. Anything he shares gets reported in the Pungent Press group."

"The what?" Kaylee asked.

"There's a whole chat group of authors and other folks he's taken advantage of. Pungent Press because it stinks, right? I'm in it because, even though Griffin himself doesn't participate, there's a lot of discussion of him and his books, seeing as how they've become so successful. Baron had been posting for a week about the gallery opening, so everyone there knew all about it. And then, I'd seen him myself in town on Monday, just walking down the street."

That was the day he'd visited Kaylee, she recalled, peddling the note cards. "But how did you know what he looked like?"

Magdalene gave her a slightly incredulous stare. "There are pictures all over the Internet."

"Of course," Kaylee said. "So what happened that night?"

Magdalene sighed. "Yes, I knew about the gallery opening, and I was mad that he got to do things like that when he treated Griffin so poorly. And I'd thought about going just to see him, maybe try to confront him. I drove in and parked by the gallery, but I just didn't have the nerve to go inside. I decided to forget it and have a walk as usual." She spoke as if she regretted her lack of nerve.

"And then what happened?"

"I walked all over town, then down to the shore and back. I had a big flashlight, but I tried not to use it. I wanted to be alone, so I didn't want anyone to notice me. And eventually I got a little confused about where I was, but I guess I must have come up on the gallery from behind because suddenly there was the back of some building, and who was standing there but Emmet Baron." Magdalene gave a rueful smile. "I thought it must be fate. Here's my chance to tell this creep just what I think of him after all. So I went right up to him and—well, started yelling at him."

"And how did he respond?"

"He seemed surprised at first. But I don't think it was the first time that something like that had happened. Pretty quickly, he was sneering at me and telling me that I should be thanking him since he's the one who discovered Griffin's books and brought them to the world. Griffin would be nothing without him, he said."

"What did you say?"

"I'm afraid I got angry," Magdalene continued, her voice going even softer. "Maybe you've noticed, but people tell me that I wave my arms a lot when I'm worked up. So then he took a step toward me. I didn't know what he was going to do, so I panicked. I just lashed out blindly. And I still had that big flashlight in my hand, and it hit him in the back of the head because he was so close. And he just went down."

"So what did you do then?"

"I ran. I didn't think he was really hurt, I thought he was going to jump back up and come after me. I ran down the alley because I could see the street at the other end, and I wanted to get where people were. Somewhere in the dark alley, I tripped. That's where I lost this, I guess." She held up the blue dragon. "I was so scared. I jumped right back up, and then I was through the alley and I saw my car down the street, so I ran to it and climbed in. And I saw two women coming out of the gallery so I started it up and drove away." If she realized that Kaylee had been one of those two women, she didn't say.

"Why haven't you come forward?" Kaylee asked.

"I was scared. I'm still scared. But also, part of me felt that he had just gotten what he deserved. Everyone was saying that it wasn't murder, that he had suffocated. I thought, 'Who would it help if I were to tell?'" She sat up straight. "But then just now, when Griffin said what he said about Baron, when he didn't complain and behaved like the better man he is—well, if he can be a good person that way, I guess I'd better try to be one too. Except then I got scared again and ran out."

"Well, you're being the better person now," Kaylee said, "and now that you've started, I'm sure you'll keep on. What do you say we go back to my shop and I'll make you some tea, and then we can call the sheriff from there. Okay?"

Magdalene put a tentative hand on Kaylee's arm. "You're so nice. Will you stay with me?"

"Yes." Kaylee laid her hand on top of Magdalene's. "Of course I will."

The next day, Kaylee indulged Bear shamelessly at The Flower Patch. "I'm going to have to go out and buy more treats," she told him, and he wagged his tail in encouragement of this plan. She had a hunch Jessica had given him more than a few extra goodies the night before, when she'd collected the dog from Albert Putnam's and taken him back to Wildflower Cottage so that Kaylee could stay with Magdalene.

After the young writer's confession, they had called and then waited together for the sheriff. With his permission, Kaylee had also gone along to the station. She'd even been allowed to stay in the conference room while Magdalene gave her statement. When it was done, Magdalene looked both exhausted and relieved, and she'd given Kaylee a long hug before being taken away. It had been late indeed when Kaylee finally made it home, but the gratitude she felt at finding her dog there safe and sound took the edge off of her exhaustion.

A good night's sleep restored her peace of mind considerably, but she wasn't bothered that business was fairly slow that day at The Flower Patch. Mary and Herb were off to Canada on their vacation, so it was just her and Bear minding the shop.

Of course, just as she started eyeing the advance copy of Griffin Graves's *The Night of the Second* that DeeDee had brought by that morning, the bell on the shop's front door chimed and Justine, Darren, and Joe Lucas entered.

Bear trotted over to greet them with a happy bark, then sat on his haunches and gazed up at Joe.

"Hello, Bear," he said. "I'm glad to hear that the threat against you has passed." He leaned down to give the dog an affectionate scratch under the chin.

Kaylee frowned. "How did you hear about that?"

Justine laughed. "We've just come from Death by Chocolate, where we also heard that you've solved the mystery of who attacked Emmet Baron."

"'Solved' is perhaps too strong a term," Kaylee said, "but the truth finally came out. What brings you by?"

"We're on our way to catch the ferry and get Grandpa back to the mainland," Justine answered. "But he wouldn't leave without coming to see Bear. And of course, we wanted to thank you."

"Well, I'm happy to have helped, but I didn't do much," Kaylee said humbly.

"You figured out what happened to Emmet, which got the sheriff off of Darren's back," Justine replied. "They came asking about what kind of car he drives, and we all got really nervous."

Kaylee grimaced. "I'm sorry, Darren. I didn't mean to give them any reason to suspect you when I told them I smelled exhaust fumes that night."

Darren waved off her apology. "It's all good."

Justine seemed to brighten as she said, "And you also seem to have convinced Mr. Putnam and Mr. Randall to help us in recovering the *Orcas Island Triptych*. We're very grateful for that too."

"They came up with that arrangement themselves," Kaylee said. "I can't take any credit there."

Justine smiled. "They don't seem to feel that way."

"So it's going to work out?" Kaylee asked hopefully.

"There are still some details to nail down, but yes, it seems likely at this point. I know Shirley would be so pleased." Justine paused, then cleared her throat. "And what about this poor woman? Magdalene, right?"

"There are also some details to nail down there," Kaylee said, "but I think the sheriff is convinced that it was an accident, and he is inclined to treat it accordingly."

The three Lucases nodded gravely. After a moment, Joe gave his granddaughter a nudge, and she in turn nudged Darren, who handed Kaylee a bag that he'd been holding loosely at his side.

"Kaylee," Justine said, "we'd like you to have this, to remember Shirley by."

"You didn't have to get me anything." Reaching into the bag, Kaylee pulled out a picture frame. Once she had cleared the tissue paper away from it, she gazed at the drawing inside the frame and smiled broadly.

"It's an early study for the triptych," Justine explained.

"It's exquisite," Kaylee gushed, her eyes roving over the

details of the sketch. "Thank you so much."

"Thank you, Kaylee," Justine said. "Let us know if there's ever anything we can do for you."

Once the Lucases left to catch the ferry, the shop was again quiet. Kaylee retrieved a hammer and nail from the work area and found a spot behind the front counter to hang the frame. She felt lucky to have the chance to see Shirley Lucas's work—art that spoke to Kaylee on a deep level—every day at a place Kaylee loved so dearly.

With the framed sketch in place, Kaylee gazed at it contentedly, then surveyed the shop. As always, there were a thousand small tasks crying out for attention, from tidying up the displays of garden tools to inventorying the flowers in the cooler to sweeping up the bits of plant matter under the workbench. But looking around, Kaylee saw that Bear had already made his way to his bed and was settling down for a nap.

She eyed *The Night of the Second* sitting on the counter.

"Well," she said, "maybe just one chapter."

Up to this point, we've been doing all the writing. Now it's *your* turn!

Tell us what you think about this book, the characters, the bad guy, or anything else you'd like to share with us about this series. We can't wait to hear from *you!*

Log on to give us your feedback at:
https://www.surveymonkey.com/r/FlowerShopMysteries

Annie's FICTION